Presented to:

_____

FROM

_____

OCCASION

_____

DATE

FOCUS ON THE FAMILY®
presents

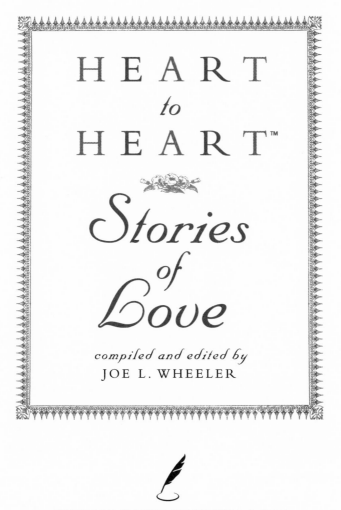

HEART
to
HEART™

Stories
of
Love

compiled and edited by
JOE L. WHEELER

TYNDALE HOUSE PUBLISHERS, INC.
WHEATON, ILLINOIS

Visit Tyndale's exciting Web site at www.tyndale.com

Copyright © 2000 by Joe L. Wheeler. All rights reserved.

A Focus on the Family book published by Tyndale House Publishers, Inc.

Focus on the Family is a registered trademark of Focus on the Family, Colorado Springs, Colorado.

This text or portions thereof are not to be reproduced without the written consent of the editor/compiler.

Woodcut illustrations are from the library of Joe L. Wheeler.

Heart to Heart is a trademark of Tyndale House Publishers, Inc.

Designed by Jenny Destree

Published in association with the literary agency of Alive Communications, Inc., 7680 Goddard Street, Suite 200, Colorado Springs, CO 80920.

Library of Congress Cataloging-in-Publication Data

Heart to heart stories of love / compiled and edited by Joe L. Wheeler.
    p. cm.
    ISBN 0-8423-1833-X
    1. Love stories, American.   2. Christian fiction, American.   I. Wheeler, Joe L.,   II. Title.

    PS648.L6 H38 2000
    813'.08508—dc21   00--024847

Printed in the United States of America

06   05   04   03   02
7   6   5   4   3   2

Dedication to

LAWRENCE ANTHONY WHEELER
BARBARA LEININGER WHEELER

Pearl Buck, in her wondrous story "Christmas Day
in the Morning" voiced this truth: "Love alone would
waken love."

I am capable of love because I grew up surrounded,
engulfed, by it. When my mother and father were together
in a room, I couldn't enter it without sensing the love that
was there. Because their Song of Solomon love for each
other was so deep and wide—anchored as it was in God—I
could blossom, for our home was built upon the Rock.

Even in his eighties, when Dad sang "I Love You Truly"
or "Smiling Through" and looked at Mom, that love for
her still blazed across the room.

Tomorrow would have been their sixty-fourth wedding
anniversary. When we phone my widowed mother and
wish her "Happy Anniversary," she will choke up and say,
"We love you."

Joe L. Wheeler
July 30, 1999

CONTENTS

ACKNOWLEDGMENTS

More extensive and exhaustive author-related research has been done for this particular collection than for any other collection I have ever put together. Hopefully, some of our knowledgeable readers can help us fill in the gaps.

"Introduction: The Many Faces of Love," by Joseph Leininger Wheeler. Copyright © 1999. Printed by permission of the author.

"Appointment with Love," by Sulamith Ish-Kishor. Published in *Colliers,* June 9, 1943. Reprinted by permission of Johanna Hurwitz, executor of the Ish-Kishor estate.

"The Man Who Played the Cymbals," by Abbie Farwell Brown. Published in *The Interior,* March 9, 1899.

"The Mistress of the Bees," by Nelia Gardner White. Published in *American Magazine,* March 1927. If anyone can provide information on the earliest publication of this old story or on White's next of kin, please relay information to Joe L. Wheeler, c/o Author Relations, Tyndale House Publishers, Inc., P.O. Box 80, Wheaton, IL 60189-0080.

"The Bashful Preacher," by Neill C. Wilson. If anyone can provide information on earliest publication and date of this story or on Wilson's next of kin, please relay information to Joe L. Wheeler, c/o Author Relations, Tyndale House Publishers, Inc.

"Home is the Sailor," by Leon Ware. Published in *Good Housekeeping,* May 1963. If anyone can provide information on earliest publication of this story or on Ware's next of kin, please relay information to Joe L. Wheeler, c/o Author Relations, Tyndale House Publishers, Inc.

"The Rocking Chair," by P. J. Platz [Patricia and Traci Lambrecht]. Originally published as "Time and Again" in *Woman's World,* January 27, 1998. Republished by permission of the authors.

"Come to the Wedding," by Jean S. O'Connell. Published in the *Saturday Evening Post,* June 8, 1957. If anyone can provide information on the earliest publication oft his story and O'Connell's next of kin, please relay information to Joe L. Wheeler, c/o Author Relations, Tyndale House Publishers, Inc.

"I Didn't Even Know Her Number," by Arthur Milward. Reprinted by permission of the author.

ACKNOWLEDGEMENTS

"Young Mrs. Richard," by Grace S. Richmond. Published in *The Youth's Companion,* April 17, 1902.

"The Trouble with Arabella," by Robert Bassing. Published in *Woman's Home Companion,* January 1955. If anyone can provide information on the earliest publication of this story or on Bassing's next of kin, please relay information to Joe L. Wheeler, c/o Author Relations, Tyndale House Publishers, Inc.

"Latch the Door Lightly," by Catharine Boyd. Published in *Redbook Magazine,* May 1960. If anyone can provide information on the earliest publication of this story or on Boyd's next of kin, please relay information to Joe L. Wheeler, c/o Author Relations, Tyndale House Publishers, Inc.

"Johnny Lingo's Eight-Cow Wife," by Patricia McGerr. Published in *Woman's Day,* November 1965 and condensed in the February 1966 *Reader's Digest.* Reprinted by permission from the February 1966 *Reader's Digest.* If anyone can provide information where Patricia McGerr may be contacted or her next of kin, please relay information to Joe L. Wheeler, c/o Author Relations, Tyndale House Publishers, Inc.

"The Slip-Over Sweater," by Jesse Stuart. Originally published in *The Woman's Home Companion,* January 1949. Republished by permission of Jesse Stuart Foundation, P.O. Box 391, Ashland, KY 41114.

"The Green Dress," by Cathy Miller. Copyright © 1990. Printed by permission of the author.

"A Song From the Heart," by Mabel McKee. Published in *Young People's Weekly,* July 22, 1933. Text used by permission of David C. Cook. Story reprinted by permission of Fleming H. Revell, a division of Baker Book House Company.

"A Rose for Miss Caroline," by Arthur Gordon. Included in Gordon's book, *Through Many Windows,* Fleming H. Revell, 1983. Republished by permission of the author.

"The Attic Bride," by Margaret E. Sangster. Published in *Young People's Weekly,* February 10, 1934. Text reprinted by permission of David C. Cook.

"The Light of My Eye," by Wang Yang. Published in *Central Daily News,* Taipei, Taiwan, July 10/11, 1973; and *Reader's Digest,* April 1974. Reprinted by permission of *The Central Daily News;* and by permission from the April 1974 *Reader's Digest.*

"When Love and Duty Meet." Author unknown. If anyone can provide information of authorship, date, and place of original publication of this old story, please relay information to Joe L. Wheeler, c/o Author Relations, Tyndale House Publishers, Inc.

Introduction

THE MANY FACES
OF LOVE

Joseph Leininger Wheeler

What is love anyhow? It is the magical ingredient that no scientist has ever been able to isolate, the yeast that can transform a friendship into love, marriage, and family.

*O*ne of my favorite definitions of love came from the pen of Washington Irving, one of America's first great writers. His only love, Matilda Hoffman, died when Irving was twenty-six. He never married but authored one of the most romantic books ever written, *The Alhambra*. The book contains one of my favorite love stories, "The Pilgrim of Love" (a little bit too long for this collection). In it, a prince who has been shut up in a palace tower learns the language of the birds, and a little dove teaches him what love is:

> "Love" is the torment of one, the felicity of two, the strife and enmity of three, . . . the great mystery and principle of life, the intoxicating revel of youth, the sober delight of age. . . . Every created being has its mate; the most insignificant bird sings to its paramour; the very beetle woos its lady beetle in the dust; and yon butterflies which you see fluttering high above the tower and toying in the air, are happy in each other's love.

One of the loveliest summations of what love is was written by my cherished friend, Arthur Gordon, in his great book, *Through Many Windows*:

> "Love . . . is a shining thing, like a golden fire or a silver mist. It comes very quietly, you can't command it, but you can't deny it, either. When it does come, you can't quite see it or touch it, but you can feel it—inside of you and around you and the person you love. It changes you; it changes everything. Colors are brighter, music is sweeter, funny things are funnier. Ordinary speech won't do—you grope for better ways to express how you feel. You read

poetry. Maybe you even try to write it. . . . Oh, it's so
many little things. Waltzing in the dark, waiting for the
phone to ring, opening the box of flowers. It's holding
hands in a movie; it's humming a sad little tune; it's walking
in the rain; it's riding in a convertible with the wind in your
hair. It's the quarreling and making up again. It's that first
drowsy thought in the morning and that last kiss at night."

THE STAGES OF LOVE

God designed us to take joy in natural stages, including the
natural stages of love.

His plan is simple but beautiful. First, we watch our parents:
the love they show to us is the love we shall pass on. Second, we
experience the love of God, which becomes the catalyst for our
philosophy of love. Third, we love the innocent and pure love of
childhood—friendship in its most disinterested form. Then there
is the love of adolescence. If we preserve our virginity until marriage (God's plan for us), this teen period will be a time for developing some of life's stronger friendships. In this time of seasoning,
of gradually developing values to live by, there is no place for
sexual passion, which can do nothing at this stage but destroy,
disillusion, and rob us of one of God's greatest gifts: coming to
the marriage bed as virgins. Adolescence is followed by young
adulthood, time for us to be blinded with the rapture of first love;
time for us to get to know each other as friends and soul mates;
time for us to compare our pasts, presents, and futures, in order to
see if we are truly compatible; time for us to see if our families
would be compatible—for we do indeed marry families; time for
us to discuss God and church and how big a role we would allo-
cate to them. Then and only then are we ready to think seriously

about marriage and family. God designed the process to crescendo as the marriage day nears, culminating in a wedding without guilt, stigma, or regrets.

Today's media leaders seem determined to destroy all of this. They sell us a bill of goods. They tell us, as did the serpent in Eden, that God lies, that instant gratification will make us gods. They tell us that modesty, virginity, purity, and integrity are for fools. They tell us that minds and hearts and souls don't matter at all; all that really matters is self-gratification, *gusto*. They tell us—over and over and over—that sex has nothing to do with friendship, love, respect, commitment, or being soul mates. Instead, they claim that sex is an acquired skill, like golf or hockey, and the more teachers we have in this respect, the better. They tell us that preliminaries are for the simple: five minutes after we meet, it's time to disrobe and show the other "how good we are" in bed!

What the media doesn't tell us is that virginity is an absolute: one can no more be partly a virgin than one can be partly pregnant. They don't tell us that Eve's first response after eating the apple was not godlike euphoria but a guilty realization that she was naked. They don't tell us that, with the sexual act, all of the illusions, all of the progressive beauty of getting to know a soul, heart, and mind prior to getting to know the body—all of that is irretrievably lost. They don't tell us that even the marriage ceremony itself is anticlimactic if we have already lived together.

Permit me to quote here from one of my books, *Remote Controlled* (Review and Herald Publishing, 1993):

> Last year in my world literature class we read and discussed Victor Hugo's *Les Miserables*. I have asked many previous classes to read the book, but it had never before elicited the

response of last year's class: "Dr. Wheeler, what naive innocents Cosette and Marius are! . . . Sitting there on a park bench day after day, just talking and looking at each other!" And for the first time it really came home to me what the media has done to our conception of love—in this case, romantic love.

There is no magic to love anymore. No hauntingly beautiful, gradual unfolding of the petals of love, leading up to the ultimate full flowering of marriage and a lifetime together. No, in today's fiction and celluloid portrayals, there are no courtships. There are in today's music and MTV, in today's advertising, not even any preliminaries! Boy meets girl, man meets woman, and bam! If the chemistry is ripe—and it apparently almost always is—before the relationship is more than minutes old, before they so much as date awhile in order to see whether or not they even *like* each other, before they so much as hold hands, before they so much as experience the rapture of that first gentle kiss . . . before any of this, within minutes they are nude and in bed with each other! This is what my students were *really* responding to in . . . the courtship of Marius and Cosette.

The truth that seems to have been forgotten in our modern era is that sexual purity before marriage nurtures and preserves the magic of romantic love.

In the stories chosen for this collection, a number of different stages of love are depicted. First of all, as in "I Didn't Even Know Her Number," there is the love shared by a small boy and girl. We adults may laugh at it and label it "puppy love," but in truth it can be every bit as intense and heartfelt as any later love. It is often purer, in a way, than later love because it is based on friendship rather than hormonal demands. No matter how old we may get, I'd guess none of us can ever forget the boy or girl we loved so deeply those many years ago. The kind of first love that can happen in childhood is often strong and enduring. And when children feel misunderstood or clouds obscure the sun of their days, their anguish can be deep. In *Island Magic,* Elizabeth Goudge observed that "children are afflicted with an acute power of suffering, thus adult counselors must be aware of the enormous gravity of the little mole hills that to their tiny stature seem such mountains."

Next, we have stories such as "The Slip-Over Sweater" that center on adolescent love. This, too, is a very special and sometimes deep type of love. It is expressed differently than either earlier or later love—by shoving, nudging, teasing, wrestling. The touch of the other is what excites, but few teens really know what to do with the sudden new drives within them. Neither do they judge maturely, for at this age peer pressure is almost God to them, and the qualities they prize most tend to be shallow. Because of our sophisticated technological society, adolescents aren't encouraged to marry as young as their counterparts of a century ago. In the agricultural economy of bygone days, many married while little more than children. The work was brutal and babies came regularly. Women looked old by their late twenties. They had no real youth but moved seamlessly from childhood/adolescence into marriage. Today, in a different economy and with user-friendly divorce laws, teenagers who marry face incredibly daunting pressures. If children come quickly, the odds against marriage survival are grim. But the real problem with such early marriages has to do with marrying for all the wrong reasons: the young marriage partners aren't even thinking of the kind of qualities it will take for the relationship to last a lifetime. Furthermore, as children themselves, they are neither ready to face the responsibilities that come with marriage *nor* those with children.

Our third-stage stories have to do with those fascinating and quicksilver hybrids: boy-into-man and girl-into-woman, ages approximately eighteen to twenty-two, as the main characters in "The Bashful Preacher." Where love is concerned, this is probably the most erratic and volatile period we know. It is also likely to be the time of our lives when that incredible condition we label "First Love" comes to us—a love that is all-consuming, leaving us with little interest in anything outside its parameters. Many marriages take place during this period, and many last. But there is a likely time bomb ticking away in any such marriage. It has to do with the maturity lag between males and females of this age—how often I have observed it in my classes! The average coed eighteen to twenty-two years old is three to five years more mature than is the male. Thus there is a real likelihood that the male will be obsessing on externals rather than the inner qualities that contribute to marriage longevity. Not until the mid-to-late twenties is the average male likely to look deeper than skin.

Then there are stories—such as "Appointment with Love," "The Rocking Chair," and "Home Is the Sailor"—that have to do with men and women approximately age twenty-three to their midthirties. Marriages that take place during this period have good odds for lasting a lifetime, for the marriage partners are mature enough to be looking for the right things but not so old that they have begun to sink into their own habit grooves. George Macdonald pointed out that "one's readiness to fall in love ought to be delayed until his individuality is sufficiently developed."

I SAW YOU TODAY

I saw you today.
I have known you all my life but I never saw you before today.

How could I have been blind to
those soft lips that shyly beckon mine,
that golden hair with fragrance of the Loire,
that adorable ski jump nose which freckles in the sun,
those slim hands which tingle to the touch,
that enchanting low-toned voice that echoes through my dreams,
that kindred mind which instinctively slices through mica to the
   gold,
that perfectly proportioned body which sends my senses reeling,
that purity of thought and naiveté
that deep abiding faith in the Father of us all.
I saw you today . . . Darling.

I have known you all my life but I never saw you before today.

"I Saw You Today," Joseph Leininger Wheeler, first published in
Roundup, 1976.

Love within marriage is totally different from love—even
romantic love—outside of marriage. Once two people *know*
each other in a biblical sense, there can be no going back to a
relationship short of that, for all relationships pick up where
they last left off. And love during the honeymoon period is
very different from love during the all-consuming period of
child rearing. Just as different is love after the children grow
up and leave home, or love after both partners retire, or love

when both partners have been crippled by the onslaught of the years.

C. S. Lewis felt the middle period of life was quite likely the most dangerous one adults face, for we find it so terribly difficult to *persevere* (concept developed in *The Screwtape Letters*) and the decades contain built-in fuses caused by boredom and sameness. Gail Sheehy, in her landmark book, *Passages,* postulated that the middle years (thirty-five to fifty-five) were the most volatile, with husband and wife likely to have grown the furthest apart they will ever be. It is also the period of life when the children leave home, the hair begins to thin, the middle begins to bulge, the career options begin to narrow, and boredom within the marriage is at its maximum. Without God to hold the marriage together, the odds are not good. If partners remain in love with what the other once was, that is a sure-fire recipe for dissolution, for each of us continues to change every day of our lives. We are totally different creatures than we were five, ten, twenty, or thirty years before. Only as husband and wife continually fall in love with the person the other is becoming is the marriage likely to retain its magic and joy. Stories such as "The Snow of Christmas" and "Young Mrs. Richards" mirror the early portion of the middle period of life, and "The Green Dress" reflects that later dangerous period.

There are other categories of stories represented as well, but I want to specifically mention one: those stories about a person whose romance and child rearing is vicarious or secondhand rather than primary, a person who picks up the leavings of others yet still counts herself blessed. In this respect, "Mistress of the Bees" is one of the most powerful love stories I have ever read.

THIS COLLECTION

I am confident that you will find reading this collection to be a life-changing experience—because the chosen love stories are the greatest I have read over my entire career. There were so many splendid stories to choose from that I found it very difficult to make any cuts. In the end, I just had to wield the knife and console myself by muttering, "If readers love these as much as I think they will, perhaps the opportunity will arise for a second collection of love stories—I can include them then."

CODA

I invite you to search out other stories of equal power, stories that move you deeply and that illustrate the values upon which this nation was founded. Many of these stories will be old, but others may be new. If you send me copies of the ones that have meant the most to you and your family, please include the author, publisher, and date of first publication if at all possible. With your help we will be able to put together additional collections (centered on other topics) for home, church, and school. You may reach me by writing to:

Joe L. Wheeler, Ph.D.
c/o Editorial Division
Tyndale Publishing House
351 Executive Drive, Box 80
Wheaton, Illinois 60189-0080

May the Lord bless and guide the ministry of these stories in your home.

APPOINTMENT
WITH LOVE

S. I. Kishor

This is a story I read once many years ago—then was unable to ever get it out of my head. I have shared it many times with students in my classes; they admit to not being able to get it out of their heads either.

It has to do with one of the deepest-seated fears we mortals have: Are we loved merely because we are attractive externally . . . or are we loved for what we are inside?

I finally found the story's original appearance after sleuthing several days in the Nimitz Library at the U.S. Naval Academy in Annapolis. As I leafed through magazine after magazine published during those dark war years, I couldn't help but notice how almost everything printed tied directly or indirectly to the war. Even the ads. Patriotism, God, the fragility of life, the likelihood that a son or sweetheart or husband or relative would never again come home alive—all gave to those magazines a moving poignancy. And this particular story, appearing in mid-1943 (two long years before the war was over), must have deeply moved those who read it then.

Six minutes to six, said the great round clock over the information booth in Grand Central Station. The tall young Army lieutenant who had just come from the direction of the tracks lifted his sunburned face, and his eyes narrowed to note the exact time. His heart was pounding with a beat that shocked him because he could not control it. In six minutes, he would see the woman who had filled such a special place in his life for the past thirteen months, the woman he had never seen, yet whose written words had been with him and sustained him unfailingly.

He placed himself as close as he could to the information booth, just beyond the ring of people besieging the clerks. . . .

Lieutenant Blandford remembered one night in particular, the worst of the fighting, when his plane had been caught in the midst of a pack of Zeros. He had seen the grinning face of one of the enemy pilots.

In one of his letters, he had confessed to her that he often felt fear, and only a few days before this battle, he had received her answer: "Of course you fear . . . all brave men do. Didn't King

David know fear? That's why he wrote the Twenty-third Psalm. Next time you doubt yourself, I want you to hear my voice reciting to you: 'Yea, though I walk through the valley of the shadow of death, I shall fear no evil, for Thou art with me' . . ." And he had remembered; he had heard her imagined voice, and it had renewed his strength and skill.

Now he was going to hear her real voice. Four minutes to six. His face grew sharp.

Under the immense, starred roof, people were walking fast, like threads of color being woven into a gray web. A girl passed close to him, and Lieutenant Blandford started. She was wearing a red flower in her suit lapel, but it was a crimson sweet pea, not the little red rose they had agreed upon. Besides, this girl was too young, about eighteen, whereas Hollis Meynell had frankly told him she was thirty. "Well, what of it?" he had answered. "I'm thirty-two." He was twenty-nine.

His mind went back to that book—the book the Lord himself must have put into his hands out of the hundreds of Army library books sent to the Florida training camp. *Of Human Bondage,* it was; and throughout the book were notes in a woman's writing. He had always hated that writing—in habit, but these remarks were different. He had never believed that a woman could see into a man's heart so tenderly, so understandingly. Her name was on the bookplate: Hollis Meynell. He had got hold of a New York City telephone book and found her address. He had written, she had answered. Next day he had been shipped out, but they had gone on writing.

For thirteen months, she had faithfully replied, and more than replied. When his letters did not arrive, she wrote anyway, and now he believed he loved her, and she loved him.

But she had refused all his pleas to send him her photograph. That seemed rather bad, of course. But she had explained: "If your feeling for me has any reality, any honest basis, what I look like won't matter. Suppose I'm beautiful. I'd always be haunted by the feeling that you had been taking a chance on just that, and that kind of love would disgust me. Suppose I'm plain (and you must admit that this is more likely) then I'd always fear that you were going on writing to me only because you were lonely and had no one else. No, don't ask for my picture. When you come to New York, you shall see me and then you shall make your decision. Remember, both of us are free to stop or to go on after that—whichever we choose. . . ."

One minute to six. . . .

Then Lieutenant Blandford's heart leaped higher than his plane had ever done.

A young woman was coming toward him. Her figure was long and slim; her blonde hair lay back in curls from her delicate ears. Her eyes were blue as flowers, her lips and chin had a gentle firmness. In her pale green suit, she was like springtime come alive.

He started toward her, entirely forgetting to notice that she was wearing no rose, and as he moved, a small, provocative smile curved her lips.

"Going my way, soldier?" she murmured.

Uncontrollably, he made one step closer to her. Then he saw Hollis Meynell.

She was standing almost directly behind the girl, a woman well past forty, her graying hair tucked under a worn hat. She was more than plump; her thick-ankled feet were thrust into low-heeled shoes. But she wore a red rose in the rumpled lapel of her brown coat.

The girl in the green suit was walking quickly away.

Blandford felt as though he were being split in two, so keen was his desire to follow the girl, yet so deep was his longing for the woman whose spirit had truly companioned and upheld his own; and there she stood. Her pale, plump face was gentle and sensible; he could see that now. Her gray eyes had a warm, kindly twinkle.

Lieutenant Blandford did not hesitate. His fingers gripped the small, worn, blue leather copy of *Of Human Bondage*, which was to identify him to her. This would not be love, but it would be something precious, something perhaps even rarer than love—a friendship for which he had been and must ever be grateful. . . .

He squared his broad shoulders, saluted and held the book out toward the woman, although even while he spoke he felt choked by the bitterness of his disappointment.

"I'm Lieutenant John Blandford, and you—you are Miss Meynell. I'm so glad you could meet me. May—may I take you to dinner?"

The woman's face broadened in a tolerant smile. "I don't know what this is all about, son," she answered. "That young lady in the green suit—the one who just went by—begged me to wear this rose on my coat. And she said that if you asked me to go out with you, I should tell you that she's waiting for you in that big restaurant across the street. She said it was some kind of a test. . . ."

Sulamith Ish-Kishor

Sulamith Ish-Kishor was born in England during the closing years of the nineteenth century. During her early teens, her family emigrated to America and settled in New York City. Ms. Kishor loved words, so writing was a natural career for her. She wrote several novels for young people, including *A Boy of Old Prague,* *The Carpet of Solomon,* and *Our Eddie,* winner of the prestigious *Newbery Award.* But of all her many books, poetry, and short stories, none is more loved than "Appointment with Love."

THE MAN WHO PLAYED THE CYMBALS

Abbie Farwell Brown

He could only play the hated cymbals, he who had so lately played first violin. But, he had lost more than fingers in that terrible accident—in recent days and weeks, he had also lost his heart to one who was the idol of the concert hall. Without her, life just wasn't worth living.

*A*mong all the seventy black heads in the orchestra, a single yellow one shone like a lamp amid surrounding darkness. This head had no business to be so conspicuous; the sight of it was an unwarranted impertinence. For it merely directed the playing of the cymbals. Yet of all the planets in that solar system whereof Herr Ritter, the conductor, was the sun, not one of them—not even Herr Ritter himself—had the musician's soul which thrilled in this meanest satellite in its orbit most remote from him.

As his name and his melancholy black eyes betrayed, despite his yellow hair Antonio Straboni was thoroughly Italian as the best of them. He detested the cymbals. He played them only because even a musician must earn bread to keep body and soul together, and this was the only instrument left him to play. For he had never even thought of seeking a livelihood through any other means than music. He had not always hung on the outskirts of the orchestra, a pariah, removed as far from the sensitive audience as the depth of the stage would allow. Once they had desired him as near as possible. Once he had sat close under the conductor's stand, and Herr Ritter had depended on him as a captain depends upon his lieutenant. For the music had received its soul from his hands. He had played first violin.

Yet everyone said how fortunate he had been to escape with his life in that fearful railroad accident when so many around him were killed outright; when he had suffered only with two maimed hands, two limber fingers gone. Fortunate indeed! Antonio envied those others, who would never know what it was to live on and on and become as sounding brass in the world's symphony. A first violin doomed thenceforth to play—the cymbals, which was but machine to him!

Yet not even his daily crashing of these brass abominations could dull Antonio's ear nor drown the music, which like a spring unquenchable, welled up within his soul. Every morning after rehearsal till it was time for dinner—which he did not always get; every night after the performance till it was time for sleep, which he did not often seek—for dreams are sad things, sad as reality when life is unhappy—he would take down his widowed violin and play clumsily, as his poor fingers would permit, the songs which had come to him since the day before; wondering the while that they should find source in his starved soul.

Kinless, friendless and alone—for his sensitive pride shunned the advances which he believed due to pity for his misfortune—he had become the saddest among them all, who was never of the gayest. He had only his violin, which he could hardly play, and his ideal, which no one shared, to make life at all worth living. And often he believed neither worth the struggle and the suffering and was tempted to end it all. This was the spirit which spoke through his violin. Antonio's songs were heartbreaking even in their beauty.

Lately, however, a new note had come into the melodies as they welled up faster than ever with a force and fire hitherto stranger to them, so that his clumsy fingers could barely follow on the trembling strings. His music had gained the masculine quality which it lacked to make it truly great. Yet must the melodies pass fleeting and forgotten, for Antonio himself had no skill nor desire to write them down, and there was no other who even guessed his talent—unless someone outside listening rapt, with hand on heart and eyes shining with delight, should remember and record.

It was now three weeks since a little German girl had joined the company, Herr Ritter's niece, the wonderful violinist whose name was emblazoned on the bill posters in colors bright as her own gold hair. Antonio had lived thirty long years. But from the day of their first full rehearsal, it seemed to him that time had just begun, a time whose seasons depended on the light reflected from that second golden head, the only one like his in that great, barren hall. Straightway the music began to ripple and eddy tumultuously through the channels of his being like a brook that rises higher and higher every day with hope and longing and reckless abandon, till it seems near to overflow and sweep all before it. And in the little hotel room next to him, Gretchen would sit and listen with hand on heart, eyes shining with delight—would remember and record.

Gretchen was advertised on the posters as a juvenile prodigy—a child musician. It was her uncle's policy, and thereby she supported a family of little cousins. For she herself was an orphan. On the great stage in her short blue dress with white sash and shoes and stockings, her yellow hair streaming unfilleted to her waist, she did indeed seem a mere child to the vast audience who came to hear her play.

But at the rehearsals, where Antonio's dark eyes had first lighted at sight of her, and in private life, Gretchen was seventeen and a woman grown. She was indeed quite old enough to understand the music of the pale young man who played the cymbals in her uncle's orchestra, and to feel a strange thrill when his burning eyes met hers.

Gretchen was proud, although she chose to room in this garret—like him, merely of course to save money for fresh concert frocks and ribbons and toys for the little cousins; and naturally she had never spoken to the humblest player of the orchestra, every member of which was prone before her feet. Yet sometimes when the orchestra was rehearsing and she was supposed to be practicing the difficult music of her evening's solo—first looking to be sure that she was quite unheard,

Gretchen would mute her violin and softly play some quaint, exquisite air surely never included in the complete works of Brahms or Raff or any of the great composers whom alone her famous teacher allowed.

One morning she met him at the head of the stairs, pale and worn, just returning from rehearsal. He stopped, turning even whiter at sight of her, and half opened his lips as if to speak words which were already burning in his eyes too plainly to need utterance. She was full of the music which she had been playing all the morning—his music. She also stopped and hesitated as if with a half inclination to speak and question him. But in a moment the spell was broken. Her pride flushed at the very thought of her indiscretion; and noting the toss of her head, he too flushed, and with a quick sigh of self-restraint passed on into his room. Halfway down the stairs she lingered a moment, listening for the sound of his violin. But it did not come, and with an impatient gesture she ran out into the sunshine and fresh air and forgot all about it.

He, however, did not forget. Late that night, after a grand performance, Gretchen was wakened suddenly by the tones of a violin which thrilled her through and through—tones bearing a new power and passion. At last the little brook in Antonio's heart had risen so high that another drop would mean overflow. It poured out in a flood of melody so divine in theme, though limping, alas! in the execution, that the girl on the other side of the thin partition was almost overcome by its beauty; trembling and sobbing with emotion, she sprang for her own violin to repeat the measures and respond, when the music ceased suddenly, and for a few minutes there was a tense silence, while Gretchen fell back quivering and nerveless with the beautiful melody still throbbing through her veins.

Then the door of the room next to hers creaked softly, and a stealthy footstep crossed the hall. A moment later she recognized the rustle of paper under her door. She kept quite still till she heard the step descend the stairs. He was evidently gone on one of the nocturnal rambles which she knew he was wont to take as a tonic after unusual musical emotion. She waited till she heard the outer door bang, then with a light she went quickly for the paper, and drawing it within, scanned it eagerly. It was a letter. The brook had overflowed at last.

"Dearest Senorita:—I cannot longer master the emotion of my soul. I must speak. I, the poor cymbal player in your uncle's orchestra. Never to speak to you or touch your hand or hope for more—I cannot longer live like this from day to day. I would rather die. I met you on the stairs this morning; our eyes met again tonight. Was I dreaming then also? I thought their look was kind. I dare not speak to you myself. I will not ask you to write me a reply. There is a sweeter way than that to hope or to despair. Let me hear it through your divine violin, Senorita. Let me know my doom tomorrow. The choice of your solo is your own—let it voice your message to my heart. I shall understand. Without love the brook of my heart will dry. With too much love it is overflowing now; let its stream unite with yours—or let mine cease forever.

> "I kiss your little feet,
> Antonio Straboni."

The girl sat paling and flushing by turns as she read the words painfully scrawled. Suddenly she bent and kissed the crabbed writing. Then with a quick revulsion, remembering the pride of her position, her recent triumph and brilliant future, she flung it on the floor, and seizing her violin, dashed into a gay Hungarian dance which she had chosen for the morrow's solo. What had she to do with this cymbal player, the mere artisan of the orchestra, though he might write beautiful songs which no one heard?

The applause following the first ensemble of the orchestra had died away, and everyone was eagerly awaiting the entrance of the young violin prodigy. The cymbals were laid weakly from one pair of trembling hands, and among all the black, close-cropped heads in the orchestra the curly yellow one alone was drooping and turned away from the right stage entrance. It was raised, however, showing a face white to the lips, as a childish figure emerged and tripped across the stage, bowing saucily in response to the storm of applause which greeted her. But she did not turn towards the orchestra while tuning her violin, as was her wont. She kept her head away; and Antonio's heart sank low within him.

Then with a toss of the golden mane over her shoulders, the strong young arm, too well rounded for a child's, swept the bow lightly, and the first heartless, gay notes of the *czardas* trilled forth like mocking laughter. The air was finished, and with another toss of the head, but without a glance toward the center where the cymbals ought to be, the girl tripped off the stage followed by a wild burst of applause. They insisted upon an encore. They whistled, cheered, and shouted "Bravo!" and would take no denial. In all this tumult she declared she would not play again. Herr Ritter begged, insisted. At last after much coaxing and many threats, she came tremblingly forth again. She also was a true musician. In the little time that had elapsed her mood had changed. She was no longer the proud, coquettish child, ready to wound, eager to show her self-importance and heart-freedom.

The bow trembled irresolutely in her hand. She hesitated as if undecided what to play, while the audience applauded still louder this new evidence of childish bashfulness. Suddenly she raised her eyes bravely, her cheeks flushed, and she began a strain never heard before by anyone in that vast hall, audience or orchestra: a strain so sweet, so tender, so full of pathos and pleading that it hushed the people into absolute silence, then rising to a height of passion that concluded with a sob and brought the great audience to its feet with a fury of enthusiasm. Herr Ritter beneath the stage and his orchestra upon it sat petrified with awe and amazement. The song of Antonio's overflowing heart-brook was indeed carrying all before it, even the world which knew him not.

But the girl looked neither at the great audience before her, nor at the flowers flung all about at her feet. For turning abruptly away from all this, with a little smile and a blush of self-confession, she sought instead the yellow head usually so easy to find among the black ones. But her smile faded, and her eyes grew wider and wider with foreboding as they peered in vain. The place of the cymbal player was vacant. What did it mean? Was it then after all too late? Had Antonio received her first cruel message but never the second kinder one? He would never know—never understand! With a terrible fear in her heart, remembering the hint in his letter, Gretchen stood staring helplessly at the vacant seat and the cymbals abandoned beside it. For she felt that he had meant what he said—he would rather die; he would die. And the audience continued to roar its empty applause for his music—but where was he?

With a sudden wild sob Gretchen ran across the stage and down the stairs past Herr Ritter who stared speechlessly at her as she fled she hardly knew whither. In her thin dress without cloak or hood, she was hurrying out into the darkness to find him before it was too late—to tell him all and beg him to return for the world's sake, which needed his music, for her sake, who needed him most of all.

She had flung open the heavy outer door when a hand from behind grasped her arm. A trembling voice whispered in her ear—"Gretchen!" And turning, she beheld the now shining eyes and blessed golden head which she believed she had lost forever.

Antonio's triumphs had almost come too late, as so many triumphs do. Fleeing from the mockery of the *czardas,* just as he was closing this same door behind him upon hope and love and life itself, he had caught the first strain of his own *romanza.* It had come at this last moment like a reprieve to the condemned to the scaffold. He could not realize it at first, the revulsion was so sudden. But the passion of Gretchen's heart answered to his own in her rendering of his soul's perfect music; and he at last was convinced.

They shared the triumph together—despite Herr Ritter's protests—hand in hand before the great audience, heart singing to heart in music which no other ears could hear.

Abbie Farwell Brown
(1881–1927)

Abbie Farwell Brown was born in Boston to a "blueblooded" family whose American roots date back to the *Mayflower.* After studying at Radcliffe, she went on to author such beloved children's books as *The Lonesomest Doll, The Christmas Angel, The Book of Saints and Friendly Beasts,* and poetry collections such as *A Pocketful of Posies, The Heart of New England,* and *The Silver Stair.*

MISTRESS OF
THE BEES

Nelia Gardner White

*J*en Culliton was feeling her years today. So much of the quilting bee discussion had to do with the past. She much preferred the future. Speaking of which, a wedge was being driven between her nephew Ollie and beautiful Molly.

There seemed little she could do about it.

*J*en Culliton had never been one to pry. She did not mean to overhear this time. She had come downstairs with the quilting frames, and, somehow, they had seemed very heavy, and she had stood a moment, too tired to go on. *I'll call Oliver,* she thought, *and get him to take them out.*

But she didn't call him. She leaned the frames against a chair and sat down, a little abruptly. She knew she shouldn't have tried to carry the frames.

It was very still in the house. She could even hear the crackling of the wood fire in the kitchen stove. It was with a little start that she looked out through the kitchen doorway and saw that the room was not empty. Beside the stove stood Molly Parsons from next door. At the back window stood her nephew, Oliver Crewe. There was a hurt in the bend of his shoulders that found an answering pain in Jen's heart.

Oliver Crewe meant a good deal to Jen Culliton. He was all Crewe, with his black hair and blue eyes and tall, lean body, and yet there was a quiet strength about him that was a very match for the strength that seemed to lie eternally in that great, awkward, beautiful figure sitting there beside the quilting frames.

So Jen loved Oliver. She was conscious often of a deep thankfulness that he was to carry on her work here on the farm.

Though she was in plain sight, Jen knew that neither of the two was aware of her. Oliver's hands were in his pockets, his eyes upon the September-golden hills.

"Well," came his voice, levelly, to Jen through the stillness, "I suppose there's no more use talking about it. We seem to have finished."

Jen could see something almost like fright come into Molly Parson's eyes. From a graceful, hoydenish child who grew still in the midst of a game of "Catch-a-thief" to listen to a lark's song, had come this woman, beautiful beyond even Oliver's boyish dreams of her, and with the lark's song come now to live in her slim white throat.

"Yes," she said slowly, "we seem to have finished, Ollie. It—it hurts to finish things with you—we've been friends so long."

"Friends?"

"Don't, Oliver. I wish I could make you see."

"I do see."

"No, you don't. You don't see how I *have* to sing, whether I want to or not. You think if I loved you enough I wouldn't care about the singing. It—it hasn't anything to do with love."

"You—you've made that clear. Let's not talk about it any more, Molly. There's a limit to what a man can bear. You'll stay for the quilting, won't you? Aunt Jen's been counting on you."

"Yes, of course, Oliver. Ollie—I—"

He turned, and Jen's heart grew tight at the hope springing into his eyes. But Molly did not go on.

"Yes?" he said evenly.

"Oh, nothing, I suppose—only, I hate to cut things off as if they'd never been. I feel like a little girl—going out into the dark."

Into his lean face the feeling came flooding.

"Molly! Oh, *Molly!*"

She made a little protesting gesture with her hands.

"Don't, Ollie. I *have* to go—even if it is dark."

He turned again to the window, did not answer. She stood hesitant, as if she wanted to go to him but could not. Jen felt that if only that still, faraway beauty of hers might be lighted into warmth, she would go. But she turned, instead, and came toward Jen in the other room.

"Aunt Jen!" she called.

Everyone called Jen Culliton "Aunt Jen," since the Crewe children had come to live with her.

⁕

Jen had risen, drawn the frames again into her arms as if she had just come downstairs with them. The red stung her high cheekbones, for she was not used to deception. She had on a blue gingham, as she always had nowadays, and a black-and-white percale apron tied around her waist. She did not shrink with the years, Jen; she was as tall, as powerful as ever.

"Where's Oliver?" she found herself saying. "Thought we'd set the frames up outside. It's going to be plenty warm, and we won't get many more days like this."

"Oliver's in the kitchen," Molly said gravely, but she did not offer to go after him. "Let me take the things out!"

She took the frames in her strong young arms and got them through the doorway. Jen did not follow her. She stood still, watching her for a long moment. Molly was looking toward the house, and there was a look in her eyes as if she were seeing it as Jen often did—the peaceful, pleasant, rambling wings, the wood smoke going straight up to the clear fall sky; but Jen knew that Molly wasn't seeing it at all. She was seeing Ollie.

Jen turned abruptly and went out to the kitchen. Oliver sat at the table, his head down on his arms, all his strength gone out of him. Jen put a big hand, with unbelievable gentleness, on his shoulder.

"What is it, Ollie?" she asked.

He did not answer.

"Is it Molly?"

He did not speak, but he reached up and drew her hand under his face. Jen felt it grow hot with tears.

"There, son, it'll come out all right," she said tenderly.

"It's all over," he said dully.

He jumped to his feet suddenly, pulled his arm in an angry, boyish gesture across his eyes.

"Dandy day for quilting," he said.

"Yes," Jen agreed, but her voice was troubled.

They put the frames up then, and Oliver and Molly Parsons laughed and joked till Jen thought she must have dreamed those moments in the kitchen. But young folks were different nowadays. She wished she could talk to Molly; but she'd never been able to of late years. Molly held you off. She'd put on so much sophistication since she'd been off studying, and Jen wasn't one to probe, unwanted. She did try to say something, though.

"Always took a sight of comfort in the farm on a day like this," she said as she spread out the rolls of cotton. "The peace of it kind of gets right into your bones this weather."

"Yes, it's lovely," Molly replied, not looking up. "But it must be lonely sometimes—so far from folks—and things—"

"I've never found it so," Jen said dryly. "Depends on how busy you keep, mebbe. I've always had to hustle. Kind of makes me mad, anyhow, to hear folks talk like that. You, especially, Molly Parsons, born and brought up in these hills. Guess you wasn't a very lonesome young 'un, was you?"

"No; but that was different. I hadn't known there was any other world."

"*Other world,* h'mph! It's all the same world, child. Same folks here as anywhere. I've met a sight of city folks up at my girl

Marg'ret's, and while some of 'em's right nice, seems to me most of 'em are strugglin' and graspin' and haven't any idea what they're reachin' for. They're hunting after happiness and content, that's what. Don't know as I've seen a single face up there like, say, your mother's, or Mis' Price's, or John Simmonses. And you can't say they stay here because they haven't got brains to go elsewhere. They've done well, all of 'em; and they're about as content as folks go in this world."

"Yes—but—," Molly began hesitantly.

"But what?"

"But you might have real work out there, too."

"True enough. But I'd want to make sure it was terrible real before I gave up my place here. The land gets to be part of you—and there aren't so many city flats you can say that about."

<hr/>

Molly stood staring down through the reddening orchard a long moment, her eyes wistful. But she pulled herself back with a little jerk.

"Well, I'll have to run home to dinner, Aunt Jen. I'll be back with Mother. Don't you work too hard."

"H'mph!" Jen said scornfully.

When Oliver came in to wash up for dinner, Jen asked, quite abruptly:

"What is it, Ollie—her singing?"

Oliver grew dully crimson.

"I see 'tis," Jen answered for him. "Well, she'll see—one of these days! I can see how, if she was maybe a little better singer, she'd be right. Some folks belong to the world, like; but Molly ain't one of them."

"She's made up her mind," Oliver said. "She thinks life would be . . . narrow . . . here; but it's more than that, Aunt Jen. Her singing's some kind of a force, driving her on. But let's not talk about it, Aunt Jen, let's not."

"All right," Jen said. "But I can remember Molly Parsons, singing to her dolls out under that maple there, and I hate to see her making a fool of herself."

"Did you want me to go down and get Grandma Price?" he asked, and Jen knew she could go no further.

They began to come then; Mrs. Laraway, old Mrs. Frazier, Mrs. Burgameyer, Mrs. Price, Allie Parsons, and Molly—all the neighbors.

"Good!" said Allie. "Glad you got things outdoors, Jen. Won't have many more good warm afternoons like this. Say, I forgot my shears, Jen! You got an extra pair?"

"My, that's a pretty pattern you got, Jen, for setting the blocks together with. It's hard to get that good, old-fashioned pink nowadays—mebbe it's just because I'm so old-fashioned myself; but seems to me there's nothing like pink calico for comforters!"

Grandma Price had come now.

"Never get used to cars as long as I live," she said breathlessly. "My land, I'm glad to set! Ollie's awful reckless, Jen; you ought to give him a talking-to."

"Oliver's a man now," Jen said. "Can't give him talkings-to any more."

"Well, I don't know but what he is. Sakes—don't seem possible! Why, it wasn't but yesterday that Joe and him was such little peelers they upset the whole neighborhood."

Jen was passing scissors and thread.

"Makes you know you're getting on in years," she contributed.

"Well, you bear your years well, Jen," Mrs. Frazier said comfortably.

Jen gave a little inward start. She had made that remark almost unconsciously. It was a stock remark. It did not apply to herself. She looked about at the pleasant, friendly faces and, for the first time, it came to her that they were not the busy, bustling, middle-aged friends of the years past; they were elderly women, all a little tired.

The discovery made her a little tired too, suddenly, and she sat down rather abruptly at the end of the frames. She looked up to see Molly, strong and slender and beautiful, threading a needle for Grandma Price. A swift feeling of resentment seemed to shake Jen.

Why, they were all getting old! Was she, too? Her hair was gray and, of course, she couldn't do the work she used to turn out; but she wasn't *old!* She'd never felt it—she'd never thought she looked it to the rest. But, just the same, maybe she did.

And yet she felt, almost fiercely, that there was a difference. She'd never thought of it before, but she did now. All these friends were glad to sit here and gossip and quilt, glad and content. They were satisfied to live in the past. But she wasn't. She liked to feel the reins of the farm still in her big hands, as they were. She still liked to drive into town and turn a good bargain. She was still, as she always had been, the head of the Culliton farm.

But as she looked about at all the comfortable faces, a feeling of wistfulness passed over her. Good, happy women, all of them, who'd done their part, and were resting now. Somehow, she had never thought of there being a time when she would rest, really rest, and yet, this fall, *she'd* been pretty tired, too. Then she was pulled out of her thoughts into their reminiscences.

"Ed's cousin Bart's pretty low," Allie said, taking a pin out of her mouth. "He's going the same way Ed's mother did—just the identical same way."

"You put in a couple of bad years with Ed's mother, didn't you?" Cora Frazier reminded Allie.

"I thought they were bad, at the time. They probably weren't. But I was just married and wanting a home of my own, and she was kind of overbearing. Do you mind the night she died, Jen? I was so nervous I got you to come over and stay all night.

"Remember about the bees? She was a great hand for the bees—she was kind of superstitious about them, and she told me to be sure and go out and knock on the hive, and tell 'em they had a new mistress—to keep on making sweet honey and not to go away. And it was so kind of still and frightening there that I felt I had to do it! You remember how you held the lantern, Jen, and I knocked—my hands was so cold they shook. Funny, the things folks used to do, ain't it?"

"Yes, I mind that night, Allie. I remember I thought the bees ought to be glad of getting you for a mistress, after Ed's mother. Sorry to hear about Bart; he's always had hard luck, seems to me."

"Yes; he wanted to go off to school, and couldn't get away; and then he got a year in the aviation during the war and wanted to go in for that, but couldn't on account of that hip trouble that come on. Well, it's apt to happen that way. Me—I thought I could never stand it if I couldn't be a milliner."

Mrs. Laraway laughed her fat, comfortable laugh.

"Well, when I was a girl some Salvation Army folks come to

town and held tent meetings, and I thought if I couldn't be a Salvation Army girl with a bow under my chin, I'd die!"

"I wanted to be a missionary," Jen confessed, with her dry humor. "I guess it was that old song, 'From Greenland's icy mountains, from India's coral strand' that done it! I was always fond of coral."

"Well," Allie said, more soberly, "guess you got your wish, Jen."

Grandma Price nodded her head in slow, authoritative affirmation.

"What?" Jen asked, startled.

"Well, you've done a lot of missionary work, seems to me. I could tell a few things."

Jen flushed.

"Well, don't," she said dryly.

"Remember Reverend Meadows? Guess you did a little mission'ry work there, Jen. Made his going easy for him, anyhow. And Flint Miller—I declare, it made him over after you brought him and his boy together again."

"And those four children to bring up—that's been a chore, if they *are* your own sister's!"

"Oh, that's been fun!" Jen said. "And they've been a lot of help to me—besides comfort."

"Yes, but they weren't when you took 'em. And you've put in some of the best teachers we ever had up this way, these years you've been on the school board. The folks around here was worse 'n heathen when it came to picking out a teacher for their young 'uns. Yes, you've certainly done your share there, Jen."

"Oh, fiddlesticks!" Jen said impatiently.

"I had some pretty tough years when the children were all

little," put in Katie Burgameyer, flushing. "Mis' Culliton saw to it they all had shoes and decent clothes for school—and she never went bragging of it all 'round the country, either." Katie gave a quick, loyal smile at Jen.

"Well, I heard something—straight from Nate's wife, too—about how Jen had a chance to put Nate to the wall when he couldn't meet payments on his farm. And Jen might well have done it too, for spite over the way he's acted about the school board; but she even let the interest go for a couple of years till he got on his feet. Yes—all in all—I'd say you'd done some pretty good mission'ry work, right on this road, Jen."

"Good land, Faith Laraway! What you trying to do? Make a fool of me in my old age? Shame on you! Molly, why don't you sing something for us? Seems as if it would sound good out here in the open. Sing something old, will you? We aren't much up on music out here; but some of the old things seem good to us yet. We'll quilt right along, if you don't mind."

Molly Parsons flushed. But she was unafraid, and she stood up in the shade of the big maple and sang to them: "Way Down upon the Swanee River," . . . and "Darling Nellie Gray."

"Used to sing those in singing school," Grandma Price put in once, with a satisfied nodding of her head. "Sing 'Annie Laurie.'"

So Molly sang "Annie Laurie," "Seeing Nellie Home," and "Loch Lomond." And the busy, gray-haired women about the quilting frame paused in their work, their eyes upon some faraway time as they listened to the clear, sweet voice of Allie Parsons's girl.

"Guess you're pretty tired," Jen said at last, gently. "But before you stop I wish you'd sing 'Sweet and Low,' Molly. Always thought a lot of that song."

Sweet and low, sweet and low,
Wind of the western sea—

Very tender and beautiful and sad, the young voice was, and Jen thought of the little girl singing to her dolls out beside this very tree. When Molly finished, it was very still in the big yard, as if they somehow all wished to prolong the sweetness of the moment. Faith Laraway pulled a handkerchief from her pocket and openly wiped her eyes. Allie's mouth twitched, as if tears were close. Jen felt suddenly that she couldn't longer bear the moment.

"Thanks, Molly," she said. "That was powerful sweet. We won't forget it for a good long spell, I'm thinking—will we, girls? You got that piece done, Faith? Guess we can roll it up then, and get it to the table. It'll be dark before we know it."

Then they were in the house, making sure everything was in their bags, coming, neighborwise, out into the kitchen to hold their hands above the fire that made the swift, crisp shadows warm.

"My, a fire feels good—especially at my age!" Allie Parsons said.

"H'mph!" said Jen, scornfully.

They came to the table. Caroline had come down from her home to help out, and she and Molly passed things. They seemed very young and childish, even to themselves. For there was wisdom about Jen's table that night—the wisdom of women who have borne children, whose children have borne children—the wisdom of women who have toiled through two score or more years to wrest a living from the land—the wisdom of women who live in the country, love it, find peace in it, and do not hanker to live elsewhere.

And, of them all, Jen Culliton was the wisest. As she sat at the head of her table, and made them all at home, there was something stupendous about her, some evidence of a grip on life that few possess, some dignity that was hers by virtue of her contact with earth, with the growing and selling of food.

"Mrs. Burgameyer, you'll have some more ham, won't you?" she said. "You didn't tell me how your boy was. Is he getting over his lameness all right? Molly, make some more tea, will you? Nothing like a fresh cup of tea for talking things over on! Cora, I haven't heard how your mother was?"

"Why, she's a little better today, Jen. She had a bad spell while we was picking the early apples. I was about tuckered out between cooking for pickers and taking care of her. Goodness knows, I'm not complaining, though. Ma's done lots for me all my life!"

"Yes, she's a good woman—the salt of the earth," Jen said.

Molly Parsons, in the doorway with the tea, felt a sudden stinging mist before her eyes. *There was such kindness in this house!* It was like a strange revelation to Allie Parsons's daughter. It was as if she had been following a vision for years, and now, almost up to it, it had grown suddenly small and gray and unworthy. But another took its place. A vision of a good woman, going her simple way, doing good to others with no ostentation, bringing fruitfulness out of the soil, doing her share in making the community better, bringing up children like Ollie and Joe and Caroline and Peter—a great woman, greater far than she would ever have been, going about seeking fame!

Jen smiled up at her gently as she set the tea down, not seeing what was in her heart, but touched, nevertheless, by the shining of her face.

After a little they all went out into the crispness of the autumn night.

"It's been a good afternoon, Jen," Faith Laraway said. "Don't know when I've enjoyed a day so!"

"Me either!" Cora Frazier said softly, as she gathered up her bag. "Seems a long time since we girls have got together like this. Wish we could do it oftener—I always feel good after!"

"Good night, Cora! Thanks, Allie, for lending me your girl, seems like she's part mine, anyhow! 'Night, Allie!"

They were gone. Jen turned to the table.

"You leave things alone, Aunt Jen!" called Caroline's eager voice from the kitchen. "Molly and I'll attend to everything!"

"All right," Jen acquiesced, in unaccustomed obedience. "Guess I'll just let you go ahead, girls. I'm going to sit down a minute; I feel kind of tired!"

But first she went outdoors to fetch a chair that had been left under the maple.

Molly, drying dishes, was the first to come to her. Molly had suddenly flung the dish towel aside.

"I've got to see Aunt Jen a minute," she said to Caroline. "Something I have to tell her!"

She had to tell her about the vision. But she did not tell her, after all.

Jen was not in the living room, and Molly went out on the porch and saw her sitting out there in the chair under the maples.

"Aunt Jen—you'll catch cold!" she called.

Jen did not answer and Molly ran to her, fell on her knees on the browning grass beside her, seized the big hands that had served a lifetime for others. But she had somehow known before ever she reached her.

About ten Molly came out into the kitchen. Oliver and Peter sat there. Peter was in Jen's old red-padded rocker by the fire, and his hands seemed to cling to the chair as if it somehow were a part of Jen. Oliver was beside the table, the light from the lamp falling on his face, bleak and agonized with its hurt.

Molly went straight to Oliver, put a hand on his shoulder.

"Where's the lantern, Ollie?"

"Lantern? What is it—do you want to go home?"

"No—Oh, no—I'm staying with Caroline! But where is it?"

He got up, hardly seeming to see her, and got the lantern from its place inside the sink cupboard, and lighted it.

"Come!" said Molly.

He followed her out the door and down through the back yard. She paused at the edge of the orchard, put a quick, comforting hand on his arm.

"Ollie—somehow—it seems *right!* She would have hated being old—and it was such a happy day—so—so much love in it! I—I think she'd have wanted it—to quit—in the harness, like this! Oh, Ollie—she was—she *is* a great woman!"

"Yes," said Oliver in a choked voice.

"She isn't really dead; she'll live in every home for miles around for years and years; she's a great woman, Ollie!"

She turned then, abruptly, and went on through the orchard till she came to the far end, where the beehives stood. She held out the lantern to Ollie and went down on her knees in the damp grass, lifted a shaking hand, and knocked gently.

"Don't go away, bees!" she said in the half-whisper of a sobbing child. "Make sweet honey for—for your—your new mistress!"

Oliver put the lantern down with one swift movement. He reached down and pulled Molly up into his arms. She clung to him tiredly, and his tears mingled with hers, and their hurt became eased, as one hurt. It was as if they were living in the midst of some terribly sweet, sad legend.

"Only, really," Molly said at last, her face tight against his, "there can never be any mistress here but *her!*"

Nelia Gardner White
(1881–1927)

Nelia Gardner White, born in Pennsylvania, wrote many stories and books set in Appalachia, and her stories tended to reflect enduring values. Her books include *The Thorn Tree, And Michael, Daughter of Time, No Trumpet before Him, The Pink House,* and *The Gift and the Giver.*

THE BASHFUL PREACHER

Neill Compton Wilson

It took only one reading for me—and this story has been one of my favorites ever since. As for my students, they love it! The setting is nineteenth-century Appalachia, perhaps a generation or two before that depicted by Catherine Marshall in Christy. *It shows with real fidelity the "early-marryin" world our ancestors knew.*

*T*he gold of a morning in late spring lay on forest and sloping meadow. Flowers prinked. Bobolinks tootled. The very young Elder Gatlin, a solitary traveler, rode the trail with a sword in his heart. It was a doleful day.

He came upon a flat where whacked-off hemlock sprays, dry as hay, and bleaching roof poles lay about on blackened sawdust. Snow and rain and wind had been here aplenty since the mighty revival meeting of a year ago. As a tabernacle of the Lord it was a sorry draggle. Plank seats were askew. The mourners' bench had backslid and was half in the creek. There were signs it had even been used for wholesale picnicking. But the litter was sodden from the rain.

Jay Gatlin reined up. The sight was in keeping with his unhappy mood. His mind ranged back. It was right here—he mused, right here that he first saw her. There were womenfolk to the right, menfolk to the left, and her pa sittin' on the sinner's bench, and her uncle creepin' toward it. There were a sight of repenters on that bench. His comrade and teacher, Elder Elisha Martin, had knocked the old Satan in them britch-sprawlin', and he had fetched a few clouts himself.

It all came back.

There had been smells here, that warm early-summer day a year ago, of hot bodies in uncomfortable stays; of lunch hampers; of fresh-cut hemlock branches overhead and fresh sawdust underfoot. Brother Martin, who'd brought Jay along for schooling as a circuit rider, was a time-scarred mountain of a man with granite-gray hair, stabbing eyes, huge shoulders, and spearing fingers. He roared, pleaded, sobbed, and grew hoarse and thirsty, and signed to his young helper to step up and pummel the devil awhile.

That was when Jay saw her. There before him she sat, not far back and on the aisle, her campmeeting bonnet making a pretty face only prettier. Her eyes pinned his and didn't leave them. While he lined out a sermon, his voice no trumpet like Elisha's, but a boyish fife-squeak, and sadly inclined to stammer, her foot went to her knee. Her shoes came off, first one, then the other. Her feet were nicely shaped. She poked them into the cool deep sawdust. Her mothers and sisters didn't see. She was about fifteen.

Brother Martin whupped the devil five times during that day's service, and he, a stuttering four. All four times she held her eyes on him, and his stammering did not lessen. Following the preaching came the baptizing. Brother Martin, whose bulk was commanding and muscular, saw to the squenching of the men and heavier women. Jay took the lighter women and children.

To the bank of Cat Track Run she came with her ma and pa and uncle and brothers and sisters. Brother Martin took her pa, and Jay plunged her mother and six young ones before he reached for her. Down she went and up she came, and there was her brown hair, peeled back and flowing wet. Her dress clung to her . . . like the skin of an apple. Her name was Lorrel Tiddany.

After the Tiddanys' baptizin' Ma Tiddany invited him to light and tie up later at the Tiddany cabin, if he found no better place to sup and sleep. Jay could think of no better place.

When his labors were over, he rode for the small gray dwelling. He found the place behind its fence, with the sweet peas peeking. He turned his horse into the pasture beside the tumbledown barn and returned to the front of the house where a row of small youngsters skedaddled as he approached. He stepped up to the open doorway.

She was seated at a quilting frame that was hinged to the rough wall. Her back and shoulders were toward him. Her dress was fresh and dry. She didn't see him.

But, of course she did see him. She turned a seam of blue stuff. Then she said, even-voiced, "Well, won't you come in?"

He entered. His shoes were squishy. She said, "Back up to the fire and dry out, Mr. Preacher. Or would you rather borrow Pa's pants?"

He did not have a rather for her Pa's pants. Though he was six foot, Pa Tiddany's pants would swamp him. So he stood to the hearth, the tails of his preaching coat spread and h'isted while she went on stitching.

Small noises sent his glance upward. Six children's faces were around the stairhole to the sleeping loft. Cried Lorrel Tiddany, "You young ones scuddle right down!"

The six scrambled down the ladder, squealing with glee, and shot out the back. A claw grabbed them. "Git," charged a voice and shut the cabin door.

Whoever had dealt with the children then came in. "This is Aunt Sabrina Vasey," mentioned the girl. "Auntie's visiting us."

Jay Gatlin felt himself being eyed from unruly hair and beardless chin straight down to mountain boots. Aunt Sabrina stated forthrightly, "Lorrel's a real peart girl, young man. Healthy. Pleasant-tempered. Plenty of boys are after her. She has nine quilts already. . . ."

"Auntie!" Lorrel's cheeks flamed.

"Well, might as well trot out the facts. Though, when I was your age, Lorrel Tiddany, I had fifteen quilts and my man all picked out, and landed, too."

"Auntie, stop!" To the guest, "Sit down if you've dried."

Lorrel's ma came in. Like her sister Sabrina, she was birdlike, but not so plump. Lorrel took the dishes from the cupboard. Jay, though careful not to stare, sensed the grace of her movements. With each reaching up and taking down, he seemed to hear Aunt

Sabrina's "Lorrel's healthy. . . . Pleasant-tempered." He added to himself, *In another year she'll be about sixteen. In another year . . .*

Pa Tiddany, rangy and freckled, thrust his head in. "Howdy Reverent. . . . Anybody want to help me do the chores?"

Jay Gatlin jumped up and went out with him. He came in, after twenty minutes, clasping firewood. When both men were washed, Ma Tiddany spoke. "Draw up, all that's a mind to."

Jay dropped to a stool at the foot of the table. While Ma and Lorrel and Sabrina brought in bowls of graveled 'taters and leather britches and boiled dough with apples, a five-year-old prowled behind Jay.

"Yadkin, light and perch somewheres," ordered Ma.

The moppet yelped at Jay. "That son of a hound dog has my place!"

Pa rose, wiped his mouth, and caught up his offspring as one would lift a fiddle. Yells from the lean-to followed. The two returned and Yadkin climbed to the bench beside his brothers.

Lorrel came and went. Her back was trim, her brown hair gathered with a ribbon, and a field flower poked into it. The young preacher put his mind to the poke sallet, corn bread, and sorghum sweetening.

Supper done, Pa and Jay settled by the fire, Jay's horse snug in the barn. Later the women joined the group. Jay and Lorrel found their stools side by side. Lorrel plaited a horsehair belt. The six young ones finished a game outside and wriggled into the circle. Pa Tiddany stabbed about for something to discuss: turkey shooting, Bide Beckett's big-headed calf; Link Yawkey's call on Shiloh Vasey—"I hear she flang a coffee pot at him."

"Thirty years unmarried," summed up Aunt Sabrina. "Hit's a strain."

Jay, the young minister, sought another topic. His eye passed over the chimney mantel and halted on a yard-long wooden tube. The tube was fixed at each end with a pewter ear.

Aunt Sabrina followed his gaze. "That's a courtin' tube. Ep, pass it down."

"Our forefolk brought it from Pennsylvania. Five generations used this old helper," said Aunt Sabrina. "It's fine around the hearth when folks are setting crowded. Gives young people a chance to spark, and nobody the wiser." She passed it over to the visitor.

He sensed Lorrel go sort of stiff.

Blushing, he took the ancient implement. He held it cautiously as if it were a gun barrel still hot from the words once fired through it. Aunt Sabrina, looking sleek and sly, went back to her darning. Jay, dreadfully embarrassed, lifted one end to his lips. The other end wandered everywhere except toward Lorrel. It scraped the nose of little Yadkin. That tadpole snatched his end of the tube and whooped into it: "You fine-haired hound dog!" Ma, Pa, and Aunt Sabrina all took a belt at him. He danced out of range, yelling, "Hit was worth it!"

"Git to bed, all you youngsters!" rumbled Pa.

There was dragging departure. Yadkins' pert mug showed at the ceiling hole. "You dassant talk sparkin' to her, you fine-haired . . ."

Lorrel laid down her horsehair plaiting and climbed the steep stair. Except for her low voice telling a story, silence reigned. She came down, keeping her face turned away. Jay was glad to the core when she was back on her stool.

At last, Pa yawned noisily and remarked, "Well, I guess it's time for bed." He went back of the fireside sitters and sat on the edge of the cornshuck mattress and dropped his boots one by one. Ma blew out the lamp, and there was a creak as a heavy form rolled into bed, and a whoosh of comfort. A creak of upsitting and Pa exclaimed. "You might set my rifle gun by me."

Ma handed it to him and he snecked it and clumped it down. Aunt Sabrina went to the shed off the living room and returned in a wrapper; there was a scrunch of goose feathers as she settled in the other bed. Ma's own garments swished off in the dark. She observed, "Lorrel, you and the Reverent will have to get along without us. He can sleep in that bed in the barn when he's ready."

A scrunch of feathers alongside Pa. And the house went still.

After an hour, Jay put fresh wood on the dogirons. Hickory and oak. He avoided sassafras, which brings bad luck. He wanted all the luck he could get his hands on. Lorrel's stool was so close to his, he could have touched her, but he wouldn't have done it for a million worlds. He felt waves of warmth flow from her, and peace, and turmoil, and pleasure too deep to endure, and torture that stung like salt. He wanted to jump and holler and run, fork a horse, and pelt away. He wondered if this was the ordinary state of a man in love. He knew beyond doubt that Lorrel was the right companion for him. Of course she wasn't ready to hear about it yet. She was too young, and any-way, she hardly knew him. And he, though an ordained pastor, needed time to ripen too. He needed time to outgrow shyness, to gain a greater understanding of womankind, that strange race which by simply crossing a room can uplift a man, cast him down, humble him, raddle him, and jounce him weak and silly. But surely in one more year . . .

He told himself he was merely being fair about it. But he knew that he, though a trained expounder, in that hour was thoroughly tongue-tied, able only to sit and sweat.

Whatever their aloneness together did to him, she on her part seemed in no hurry to end it. Nor did she bother to speak. The courting tube lay on the floor. Once or twice she stirred it idly with her foot. Her bedplace, he supposed, was beside Aunt Sabrina. She made no move to go to it. No sound whatever came from above. Rumbles rolled from Pa, burbles from Aunt Sabrina. The moon slanted in the door.

Lorrel gave up toeing the wooden tube; she fingered her dress. Jay caught a whiff of May pinks and crushed roses.

I'm going to unlock my jaws, he decided. *She's only a child tonight, but girls grow up lickety-fast. I'm going to speak.*

Her slim hands clasped one knee.

He reached for the courting tube. He lifted it.

He placed it to his lips, but decided to try some exploring sounds first. From bird calls he'd move with growing sureness to the valiant sounds of the human male. So, softly, he tried the tootle of a bobolink as he'd heard it on the trail. He followed with the chuckling whistle of a bobwhite. Gaining boldness, he launched the loud gobble of a wild tom turkey.

Pa's heels spanged the floor. Pa hit the square of moonlight, rifle butt at shoulder. He spun about, aiming at the ceiling, shouting, "Where's it at?"

"Things are all right, Pa!" screamed Lorrel. "He didn't even kiss me!"

Clamored Ma, "Ep, don't you pull that trigger! There's six young ones up there. I mean Tiddanys, not turkeys!"

Pa lowered the gun, looking shamed. "What kind of sound was the young man making, Lorrel? It sounded way off the p'int."

"He was following his own sweet rather, Pa. Hunting instincts took him."

Jay, shaken, saw that the wooing moment was over. He'd have to practice those stumbly words to the rocks and trees same as his sermons, and say them all to her when he came again. He stammered a hasty good night to all and went out to the barn where his horse was chomping hay from where he'd meant to make his bed.

Next morning, Lorrel seemed a mite strange to him. She looked amused, scornful, put-out, hurt—but also breathtakingly pretty with that clear red in her cheeks.

For the twelve months following, Jay rode circuit, the last half year by himself, when Elder Martin took a pastorate at Marianboro. By stormy height and sunny, by bare lane and leafy, Jay rode alone—yet not alone, for in all his thoughts Lorrel rode with him, and for the past few weeks he'd been pushing for Cat Track Hollow, knowing what he would say and must say. He was now a wise nineteen and Lorrel a grown-up sixteen.

And then he met the doctor. "They want you in the Hollow for a sight of weddings, Brother Gatlin—six of 'em, counting the Tiddanys."

"The Tiddanys! Who's bein' married at the Tiddanys', Aunt Sabrina?

"Why, Lorrel is," said Doctor Feeler. "To Beech Trevitt. Pretty girl, isn't she? Really blossomed out, the past year. . . . Are you all right?"

"Yes, quite all right."

The doctor, after giving him a quick look, jogged rapidly down the trail.

Five weddings Pastor Jay Gatlin performed in the valley, and now he was riding to the Tiddany house to perform his sixth. There were horses and wagons tethered to the fence and trees, and on the porch was a row of youngsters.

Jay dismounted and tied his horse. He was in split-tailed

marryin' coat and clean overalls. He passed the youngsters—
Yadkin grinning—and entered the house. The quilting frame was
gone. The courtin' tube was hung up by the fireboard that was
decked in flowers. Many a neighbor was there—Granny Hite,
Link Yawkey and his fiddle, a number of Trevitts.

Said Aunt Sabrina Vasey, "You should have talked through the
courtin tube, young man. You were too dilitary."

Whoops and yippees sounded and the clatter of hoofs. A band
of youths, mounted on anything with four legs and a mane,
pounded around the fenced garden, blossoms in their hats.

"He's arrove," announced Pa Tiddany, "Beech Trevitt."

The young men tied their mounts, and stormed in. Jay had
his first look at the rooster who had won Lorrel Tiddany. Beech
Trevitt could do with fewer pimples on his face, but he was
going to be a big man when he filled out. *I guess Lorrel will be
very happy,* thought Jay. . . *I guess she will.*

"Let's get on with it," pressed Pa Tiddany. "Link, raise some
music!"

Jay Gatlin took stand before the fireplace. There was a hollow
in him as big as an uprooted oak. Resolutely, he opened his
book. For all his recent practice, its pages swam. Well, he'd do
the best he could.

Beech Trevitt, Victor, and Norvill Cornett, best man, took
their places; Aster Tiddany took the bridesmaid place. Then came
Lorrel, her hand on her pa's arm. Lorrel in her wedding dress.

Beech sucked breath and trembled. Norvill sucked breath and
trembled. Jay braced himself. This was Lorrel, after one year. The
flowers in her hand quaked a little. Her downcast eyelashes flut-
tered. Her eyes lifted to Jay's.

Not all the martyrs of the church are dead.

His throat choked. His eyes blurred. But though a defeated lover, he was first of all a minister.

"Dearly beloved, . . ."

Norvill Cornett was going to ruin this service yet with all that shakin'.

Jay went on with the ceremony, fighting down a groan.

"If any man can show just cause why these persons may not be lawfully joined together, let him now speak."

Norvill Cornett yelped, "I kin show just cause!"

Pa Tiddany leaped as if stung. Ma and Aunt Sabrina's mouths fell open. Lorrel gasped.

Beech Trevitt swung around. His face was all jaw. "Who says that?"

"I say it." Norv's cry was a man's in pain.

Jay Gatlin thundered to Norv, "Speak now or forever hold your peace."

"I'll tell you why they mustn't be joined," hollered Norv. "I love Lorrel myself."

Beech swore. Aunt Sabrina screamed. Ma squeaked. Uncle Clinch shouted, "Aim for the chin, boys. Always the chin!"

Lorrel stared mutely from one man to the other, her wide eyes growing wider. The bunched flowers toppled from her hands.

Howled Beech, "I'll beat the whey out of you for this, Norv Cornett! Right now. We'll settle this outside."

"I'm willing," stated Norv, white and eager, as they started for the door.

Lorrel swayed. Jay grasped her before she sank. He swung her around. His eyes sought hers, and hers were as he'd seen them on that morning of his departure a year ago. Searching. Questioning. And at that instant he understood. "Lorrel!"

Words he'd struggled for in the courting tube and uttered the past year in a score of cabins came to him at last. Now they rushed in a torrent, with a least mite of change.

"Lorrel, wilt thou have this man, which is me? To love, cherish, honor, and sustain, in sickness as in health, in poverty, as in wealth—do you so promise?"

"I do! Oh, I do!" wailed Lorrel.

"Will I, Jay Gatlin take you, Lorrel Tiddany—will I promise to love and cherish you until death do us part? I will! By purely I will!"

Manful strife could be heard outside. Thuds, whacks, grunts. Uncle Clinch and Yadkin cheering, and Pa yelling to "punch fair!"

Ma and Sabrina were within in shocked embrace. Jay was in an embrace too. He and Lorrel broke apart, viewed each other unbelievingly, nodded fervently, embraced again; and Beech Trevitt strode in. His sleeves were gone. His suspenders split.

"We'll get on with the marryin'," he ordered.

"Beech, you're too late. The preacher has treed your coon," chirruped Aunt Sabrina. "If she ever was your coon."

Jay didn't speak. Lorrel didn't speak. They stood hand-locked. It would do until they could get over the hills to Marianboro and Pastor Martin who would lock them even tighter; and a beautiful day it was for the joyful canter.

Together on one saddle.

Beautiful spring!

Neill Compton Wilson
(1889–1973)

A man of action, Neill Compton Wilson of Sebastopol, California, climbed most of the western mountains, ran most of the rivers (including the Salmon and the Colorado), and traveled all over the world. He was also a reporter, Associated Press editor, advertiser, and freelance writer. Among his books are *Treasure Express, Silver Stampede, Southern Pacific, The Nine Brides and Granny Holt,* and *The Freedom Song.*

HOME IS
THE SAILOR

Leon Ware

"*You've let that limp spread some, haven't you? It's reached your mind, too. It isn't in your heart, though.*"

Tough words from a sailor to a librarian. But they had to be said.

She had no idea how long he might have been watching her—as a children's librarian Ellen rarely had time to notice adults. She had finished her storytelling session and ushered out sixty bubbling, happy youngsters, helped the half-dozen who remained behind to find the books they wanted, and then returned to her desk. As always, she was impressed by their breathless acceptance of her twice-weekly effort, and, as always, the experience left her glowing with pleasure. Reluctant just now to settle down to cataloguing again, she looked up and let her gaze wander out into the main reading room. He was smiling at her over the top of a thick book.

The San Diego library usually had a quota of sailors, so his being in uniform wasn't distinctive. When Ellen first saw him she thought for a long moment that he was looking beyond her. Then she realized the smile must be meant for her, and she glanced down quickly.

Men had often smiled at her—when she was seated. It was when she stood up and walked and her limp became apparent that they either looked quickly away or their expressions became charitable. She didn't like either their sympathy or their embarrassment.

At twenty-six Ellen Down had adjusted to her handicap; at twenty-six she had ceased to kid herself that a normal life was possible. Now she pressed her lips together and concentrated on her work, and the ache in her polio-shortened left leg came surging up out of her subconscious again. It was always there; she never really got used to it, but she had learned to more or less ignore it until something like this happened to remind her that a man's smile was only perfunctory.

She felt a touch on her arm and turned her head quickly, meeting the stricken look of a little girl who stood fearfully beside her, blue eyes glistening with the beginning of tears. "Oh, lady—I didn't mean to, really. I just turned the page and it tore." Nervous hands held out the dog-eared book, a page of which was almost ripped loose.

Impulsively, Ellen slipped her arm around the child and hugged her briefly. "Honey, don't you mind. We can fix that easily. Watch." She used strips of transparent tape skillfully to mend the tear. "It probably had a little tear already. So many children have read this book, it's a wonder it holds together at all!" She handed it back with a smile. "There you go."

The girl beamed. "Oh, thanks! Thanks so much!"

Ellen watched her go back to a low table, the slim, straight legs deeply tanned below the white shorts. About to turn back to her work, she lifted her eyes again.

The sailor rose just then and walked to a nearby stack—620, Engineering—to replace his book. He was tall and loose-limbed, and his long face was tanned. There was the badge of a radarman, first class, on the left sleeve of his white jumper above two red stripes that meant at least eight years of service. He turned suddenly and caught her watching him and smiled again, then walked away. Ellen looked down hurriedly, angry with herself.

Moments later she remembered to glance up at the clock. It was after four and she was through for the day. She straightened the desk, got her purse, said her good-nights and stepped through the big doors into the sparkling afternoon sunlight.

The sailor was waiting.

"Hi," he said companionably. "I knew you were off at four, so I waited to see if I could drop you some place."

He had a homely sort of face that hardly went with his confident air. There really wasn't any wolfishness in his manner, but still, he was a sailor, and a girl in San Diego saw a great many sailors.

"I beg your pardon," Ellen forced herself to meet his gray eyes with all the chilly reserve she could muster. The gray eyes remained cheerful.

"I'm Bill Farrell," he told her. "I've just been transferred to the Anti-Air Warfare School out on Point Loma and I don't know anybody who could introduce us, so I asked and you're Ellen Donn." He grinned, a slow, wry expression that revealed even teeth. "It isn't very formal, I'll admit, but it's about the best I could do under the circumstances. May I give you a lift?"

"I can manage, Mr. Farrell," Ellen said stiffly. "I can manage very well. Thank you."

She nodded with what she hoped was just the right amount of propriety—there wasn't any reason to be angry with him, only with herself for the confusion she felt—and went on toward the bus stop near the corner. It seemed as if her limp became more awkward with each step, and suddenly she hated herself for the wave of self-pity that engulfed her.

Her bus arrived almost at once and Ellen boarded it gratefully, taking a seat on the aisle. As she turned to sit, she glanced back toward the library, but he was gone. He would be, of course. She had cut him down unmercifully, and only an idiot would still be standing there.

He wasn't an idiot, certainly, even if he *was* forward. A radarman, first class, was an electronic specialist, and if he'd been transferred to the school at that rank it meant he was instructing there. Regardless of your interests, when you lived in a navy town you automatically absorbed a good deal of information about the fleet. You knew, for instance, that a first-class petty officer with over eight years service was close to becoming a chief. And even a children's librarian knew that it was the chiefs who made the navy tick.

Bill Farrell. It had a nice, unpretentious sound about it, a solidity. It went with the gray eyes and the wry grin and the startling directness of his approach. And she had slashed out at him impulsively at first sight, hardly thinking. Ellen stared ahead in the bus. Her leg ached and she despised it for what it was doing to her, for the fence she had let it build around her.

She stopped at the neighborhood market and bought cat food for Toby, a small chicken, and a few groceries. If she waited until it was quite dark to eat, the candlelight reflecting on a crystal goblet sometimes eased the loneliness of her meals. She could crumb the chicken and put it in a slow oven and then work in her rose garden until dusk.

Ellen was increasingly glad she had kept the small house when her mother died. Her first impulse had been to sell it and move into an apartment, but now it offered a continuing interest in her life. This part of her living, at least, could be normal—if living alone was really normal. When she was older, of course, it would be even easier, because it wasn't at all unusual for an older woman to live alone.

She had Toby, of course, and he was a cat whose companionship was generally comforting. But Toby managed to spoil this evening. Ellen sat at the table before the crisp chicken and reached for the thin-stemmed glass. As she lifted it her gaze fell on Toby in the big chair, his black tail curled around his white feet. He was watching her unblinkingly, reproachfully.

"And what's the matter with you?" she demanded.

Toby's eyes left hers, moved deliberately across the table to the empty place opposite her and then back again. What Ellen thought she saw in his expression could only have been her imagination, the product of self-recrimination, but if ever a cat looked disgusted it was Toby.

She put down her drink, untasted.

"I can't *help* it!" she said sharply. "I don't *want* anybody feeling sorry for me! Ever . . . *ever!*"

She pushed back her chair and half rose, then sank down again, shaken. She wasn't being intelligent or even rational. If she had reached the point where the gaze of a cat could upset her, then she was in a bad way indeed. Of course, she thought with sharp, saving amusement, Toby was by way of being a bawdy, free-wheeling type of cat. To him, at least on the basis of many neighborhood reports, being lonely was something of a sin.

"You just run your life and I'll run mine," she told him with some exasperation, feeling a little silly at this seeming need for defending herself.

She ate the chicken and sipped from the iridescent goblet, but the edge of romance had gone from the candlelit meal. It was all make-believe anyway; at times she could savor and enjoy it, but not tonight. Tonight she was just another spinster, playing at some sort of a foolish game. She washed the dishes, ran her eyes over the television schedule just in case there might be something of interest showing, and then opened the back door for Toby.

He purred, rubbed caressingly against her leg, and went on out to the porch.

"Have fun," Ellen told him bitterly.

Toby sat down on the back step, looked up at the thin sliver of moon, and licked his chops.

The greatest joy of being a children's librarian was the moment when a youngster discovered the excitement of books, and when it happened to one of the few children she knew well, it was particularly gratifying. Tommy Rodriguez was ten, a bright-eyed boy who lived on the same street as Ellen. When his class had paid the library a visit, he had been utterly delighted to find Ellen there and had taken readily to her selections for his reading. Now on vacation, he was devouring books, and because the bus line went directly from his street past the library, his mother let him make the trip almost daily. Sometimes he came late enough to ride home with Ellen.

On this afternoon Tommy stood at her desk, his eyes wide, and the story of *Treasure Island,* which he had just finished, came tumbling from his lips. He was full of pirates and pieces-of-eight and Long John Silver, and if she'd let him, he would have related the whole wonderful tale right there. Ellen laughed and rumpled his unruly black hair.

"You'd better try *Kidnapped,*" she told him. "It's not the same sort of thing, but it's by the same author, and that's often a good way to read. Come on, let's see if it's in."

As they crossed the floor, Ellen's glance swept to the outer reading room. The sailor was there again at the same table, smiling at her over what might have been the same book. She flushed and turned quickly away, and the ache in her leg, which had been forgotten in Tommy's enthusiasm, came up again.

They found the book together, and she sent Tommy on his way. Moments later she thought to ask him to wait for her, in case the sailor would stop her again, but when she looked for the boy, he was gone. So was the sailor. Ellen studied the empty place at the table with curiously mixed emotions, a little surprised that she seemed to feel some disappointment in his departure.

But when she left for the day, she found them both outside. Tommy sat on the bottom step, his foot in his hands, rocking back and forth with obvious pain. Bill Farrell squatted compassionately beside him, glancing up soberly when Ellen hurried to them.

"Looks like he twisted his ankle or something," Bill Farrell said. "I offered to take him home but he said you lived near him and would help. How about me driving you both?"

Ellen ignored him for the moment and knelt beside the boy. "Oh, Tommy! Does it hurt so?"

Tommy Rodriguez screwed up his face. "Pretty much," he admitted manfully.

Ellen brushed the straggling hair back from his forehead. "Can you stand on it?"

Tommy looked up briefly. "I dunno. Maybe I better let him drive me home, huh?"

"Well, let's see if you can walk on it first. Now—"

But Bill Farrell didn't wait. "I'll be glad to, boy," he said and slipped his arm under Tommy's legs and lifted him easily. Passersby stopped to look on curiously. Bill Farrell nodded down the street. "Maybe you'll open the car door for me?" he asked Ellen.

It was an old car, weathered from exposure, but kept clean inside. Tommy sat between them, completely absorbed in his book. As the blocks slid by, Ellen hardly heard Bill Farrell's easy chatter because it was growing on her that there was something very fishy in this whole affair. For a boy in pain, Tommy was far too relaxed. Ellen finally folded her hands in her lap and looked down at him, conscious of the mounting tension in her jaw muscles.

"How's the foot now?"

"Huh?" Tommy blinked up at her. "Huh? Oh, *Oh!* It's better. It's a *lot* better."

She had been had, definitely. Within Ellen annoyance fought a standoff battle with amusement.

"Just as soon as Mr. Farrell has carried you into your house, we'll have your mother call the doctor to come and give you a couple of shots," she said pleasantly.

"Heck, no!" cried Tommy. "My foot doesn't hurt that bad! Gee whiz!"

"Oh, but it's always best to have a shot or two," Ellen went on placidly. "Tetanus or something terrible might set in." She turned her head. "Isn't that right, Mr. Farrell?"

His eyes met hers briefly, and he smiled slightly before he turned his head away. "Well, like they say: You can carry some things too far."

"You ought to be ashamed of yourself!"

He grinned without looking at her. "They also say all's fair in love and war."

A retort died on her lips, and she felt shaken and confused. Then Tommy glanced slyly up at her, and the surge of annoyance returned. Ellen put her hand on the door handle.

"I'll get out right here, please!"

"Now, what's wrong with giving you a ride?" Bill Farrell asked.

"It's not the ride," she said spiritedly. "It's the way you did it. Using Tommy!"

Bill laughed and dropped his hand onto Tommy's knee. "Tommy didn't mind. He's all ham anyway."

Tommy giggled. "Did I fool you, Miss Donn? Did I really?"

Ellen looked down, and the mischief she saw in the bright, dark eyes touched a responsive chord somewhere within her. She suddenly wanted to pull his ears and give him a fierce hug, but she smiled faintly at him instead.

"You fooled me. You took advantage of me. I don't know very much about boys."

"You ought to give them some study," Bill Farrell said, not turning his head.

"I feel my education is now complete," Ellen told him briskly.

"Turn right at the next corner. Tommy's house is the fifth on the left."

Bill slid from under the wheel to let Tommy crawl through, but Ellen got out of her side also. Bill glanced at her.

"I'll take you home."

"I can walk from here. Thank you very, very much for the ride."

Bill patted Tommy's head. "So long, Tommy. I'll see that you get an Oscar." He looked again at Ellen as Tommy ran toward his house. "It's early. May I call on you?"

She had moved to the sidewalk as awkwardly, she thought, as she had ever walked. She lifted her chin.

"Why?"

"Why?" Bill stared at her. "Does there have to be a reason? Can't a guy call on a girl just because he'd like to?"

Her eyes faltered and Ellen looked away. She couldn't bring herself to tell him right there, bluntly, that nobody in his right mind would go calling on a cripple when a city the size of San Diego was full of normal, healthy, pretty girls. Girls who could run and walk straight and stand tall. Girls whose legs were long and even, unmarred by the scars of operations. Girls who never even thought about their legs unless they stubbed their toes. Girls who—she lifted her head.

"It's the third house," her voice seemed thin and hesitant, "on the other side of the street."

He sat on the back steps, a glass of iced tea in his hand, watching in amusement as Toby tried vainly to get his ears scratched by rubbing noisily along Bill's thigh.

"Go to it, boy—keep it up. If I give in and pet you, you'll lose interest and walk off without another glance. But keep on trying."

Ellen laughed a little. It was easier than she had thought it would be, having him there. Bill Farrell had been enthusiastic about the small house and talked easily about books and joked over the radar classes he taught and just now had complimented her extravagantly on the pleasant backyard. It wasn't often that Ellen just sat and looked at her handiwork. It *was* nice.

"Keeping it up must make you hustle," he said. "There's a lot of hard work in a yard like this."

"I like it. I have the time and this is one thing I *can* do."

There it was again, almost on the surface. Bill ignored the comment and drained the glass. He swirled the ice gently, then nodded down the yard.

"A charcoal grill, I see. Would it upset anything if I got some steaks and we dined alfresco?" He turned his head, and his gray eyes were steady. "Or would you rather go out somewhere for dinner?"

She sat quietly, hardly breathing, gazing down the shady lawn. She couldn't tell him that she had never been out to dinner with a man—parties, yes, but never to dinner alone. All the boys and all the men she had ever known had treated her like a friend, a sister—someone to confide in or bring their troubles to, but not to take out to dinner. You didn't waste money on someone who couldn't dance, who couldn't wear high heels, who limped. Long ago she had given up looking at herself in the mirror—it was a pretty enough face—and crying and asking why. She knew why. It wasn't a secret; it was there for everyone to see.

Just once, she thought now in blind confusion, just once it would be nice to go out to dinner with a man. But then it would probably turn out as Bill had said it would with Toby: Pet him and he'd walk away without a backward glance.

Yet, it might be all right here in the yard. She often barbecued for herself, and this wouldn't be much different, except that it would be much more interesting and not at all lonely. She realized he was waiting for an answer and turned her head slowly, forcing a smile.

"All right," she said. "That'll be fine. I can make a salad and some garlic bread."

"I didn't think you were going to get back," he said quietly. "I thought you'd gone off forever." He stood up and smiled—suddenly, happily. "I'll walk to the corner. Is there anything else we need?"

Dusk had deepened into night by the time they had finished eating. A leaf wobbled down from the walnut tree overhead and disappeared in the deep shadows beyond the small table. Bill hadn't wanted candles—candles were for inside, he had said—and Ellen had to agree that it was more pleasant just like this, sitting in the growing darkness and watching the stars come out. Bill filled the thin goblets, held his up against the sky and sighed.

"Perfect," he said. "Or it will be when we get some coffee."

She awoke to her responsibilities as a hostess and started to rise. "I'll start some—"

He put his hand on her arm, checking her. She felt the warmth and roughness of his palm, and gooseflesh studded her arms and the back of her neck. She sank down in her chair, and he took his hand away slowly.

"We'll go out some place for coffee."

"Oh, no," she said quickly.

"Why not?"

"I'm not dressed to go out."

"You look good enough to go anywhere, but if you want to make it some fancy spot, I'll wait while you change. But this monkey suit of mine isn't any dinner jacket."

"You look fine," Ellen said quickly. "But I—well, I don't dress up much because I can't wear high heels."

There, it was out in the open.

"So what difference does that make?"

The door was ajar and her chagrin was so great that in that unguarded moment all the years of frustration seethed up and broke loose.

"Difference? It makes all the difference in the world! Nice dresses are made to be worn with heels, not the flat things I have to wear. Nice dresses and nice places are for people who can run and walk and dance, not hobblers! That's why I didn't want to go out to dinner tonight. I wasn't ever going to tell you, but that's why. I wouldn't know how to act because I've never, *ever*, been out to dinner with a man alone!"

And then she was sobbing, holding both hands to her eyes and covering the hot tears on her cheeks, feeling utterly ashamed.

Bill sat in silence while she set her lips and choked back the tears and gradually got control of herself again. It wasn't until she had used the napkin he had offered her to daub at her eyes that he finally spoke.

"All through?"

His tone shocked her. She lowered the napkin and stared at him through the darkness.

"You've let that limp spread some, haven't you? It's reached your mind, too. It isn't in your heart, though. I've watched you for a week—eight days—and the way you handle kids, the little things you do for them, is wonderful. All those youngsters in the storytelling groups adore you. You couldn't do that to them if you didn't love them, every one. You ought to have some of your own."

There wasn't anything she could say or do except gaze at him, stunned by his almost unbelievable brutality. And then his voice softened.

"This is a pretty odd way to begin a courtship, but from the very first day I saw you, I thought you were the kind of a wife a guy like me ought to have. I'm going to stay in the navy, Ellen. I'm going to be at sea a lot of the time, but that doesn't mean I don't want to have a regular home and a wife and kids.

"Mine isn't the homeliest face in the world, but it'll do until another one comes along. This is a pretty shoddy thing to say, I suppose, but when I first saw you, and saw you limping but handling the kids the way you do, I thought you'd be the one wife who'd be home where you belonged when I was at sea. The only apology I can make for thinking such a thing is that I didn't know you at all then. By the time I finally got up courage to speak, I had long since realized that it wouldn't have made any difference if you could run like a deer; you'd be home."

He reached out again and put his big hand gently on her arm.

"So now that I've got the cart before the horse, will it be all right if I hang around and get better acquainted?"

The stars beyond his head had broken loose and were swinging frantically before her eyes. Ellen tried desperately to get a full breath into her tight chest and then dropped her eyes to look at his hand, just faintly visible as it rested on her arm. In the long moment of silence she heard only the hurried beating of her heart, and then a cricket chirped.

She found she could speak. "I—I think I'd like to go out some place for coffee after all. Some really fancy place. If you'll wait, Bill, I'll put on my very best dress."

The steady, growing pressure of his hand was all the answer she needed. It was all she would ever need from now on. The ache in her leg seemed to drain away.

Leon Ware

Leon Ware, Hollywood scriptwriter, novelist, short-story writer, and librettist, wrote prolifically during the thirties and forties, authoring such works as *Shifting Winds, Mystery of 22 East, The Threatening Fog,* and *The Jade Monkey Mystery*.

THE ROCKING
CHAIR

P. J. Platz

It was just an old rocker—so why on earth would the tall young man offer a thousand dollars for it?

More important, why would the young woman sitting on it turn him down?

*M*olly was sitting in the foyer, trying to rock away her aching back in the very chair that had caused it. She'd managed to drag it all the way down from the attic, but she was beginning to wonder if she'd find the strength to take it down the front steps and out to the truck she'd borrowed.

No wonder it had sat up there all these years, she thought. For all its beauty, the chair was almost too heavy to move. And yet it was the only thing Molly wanted from this old Victorian house that had been her grandmother's home for every one of her eighty years, and her great grandmother's before that.

She looked up and forced a polite smile as a cluster of people passed by on their way to the front parlor. The eager antiques hunters had come in a steady stream since morning, braving icy roads just to preview the items that would be auctioned off tomorrow. All of them were eager to bid on Victorian pieces her own grandmother—now happily residing in a seniors' community—could hardly wait to be rid of. Funny, she thought, that what they put such value on was of no interest to her, while this plain wooden chair was worth more than all the rest in her eyes.

She closed her eyes, letting the motion of the rocker take her into the last century. What a time that must have been, she thought with a sigh, longing for the kind of romance and the kind of man who had won her great grandmother's heart more than a hundred years before.

"Excuse me."

Molly jumped. For just an instant, she almost believed she had traveled back in time: The man who stood before her actually looked a little like the cracked sepia photograph of Tommy Buchanan hidden in the secret compartment of the chair she sat in. He was tall and broad-shouldered, as Tommy had been, and he had that same darkness about his face. Molly blinked to dispel the notion, bringing into focus a thoroughly modern man wearing a parka with a cell phone tucked in the pocket, jeans and work boots.

"Sorry," she said. "I must have dozed off."

"Small wonder. You've obviously had a very busy day." He smiled, his blue eyes crackling with intensity. "I'm sorry I startled you."

Now that she really looked at him, he didn't resemble Tommy Buchanan at all. His hair was dark, not light, and his features were stronger. Molly sighed and pushed herself up out of the chair.

"Can I help you with something?" she asked.

He nodded. "Actually, you were sitting in the one piece I wanted to examine."

Molly's eyes followed his gaze to the chair, which was too plain to earn a second glance from any serious aficionado of Victorian furniture.

"It isn't in the auction catalog," she told him.

"I know," he said. "That's why I'm here today. I was hoping to buy it outright. I'd be willing to give you five hundred dollars for it."

Molly smiled quietly at the stranger's offer.

"How about seven-fifty?" he asked eagerly.

She blinked in disbelief. "But that's ridiculous. . . ."

"I could go as high as a thousand," he offered.

Molly looked down at the chair. According to the appraiser, it was only worth a few hundred at best.

"Listen, I'm really sorry, but the chair isn't for sale," she said.

The man looked crestfallen. "Could you call your employer and present the offer?" he asked.

"My employer?"

"The auction house."

Molly sat back down in the chair as if she could protect the rocker with her own weight. "I don't work for the auction house. This chair belonged to my great grandmother, and now it belongs to me."

He took a breath and gazed at her, searching her face as if he expected to find something familiar there.

"Then the chair is yours to sell," he said softly.

Molly sighed. "That's true, but I wouldn't sell this chair for a million dollars, and, frankly, it has very little value. It was built by a man who wasn't even a furniture maker, let alone a famous one. He was just a poor, unknown carpenter."

The man's laugh puzzled her, and she marveled at the way amusement changed his face. Suddenly, she found herself wishing she weren't wearing cobwebs in her hair and the dust of the attic on her sweater.

"What's so funny?" she asked.

He shrugged amiably. "That we both desperately want this chair that's apparently worthless."

Molly stiffened a little. "You don't understand. It isn't just a chair. . . ." Her sentence trailed away, and she looked up at him.

His eyes flickered with interest. "Then what is it?"

Molly exhaled and then faltered. What was she going to tell him? That the century-old story behind this simple rocking chair brought tears to her eyes? That to her, it represented the last bit of romance in a world that had somehow forgotten it over the years?

"If you really care to know," she said, "this chair was made for my great grandmother by a man she loved but wasn't allowed to marry. His family was poor and hers was rich, and in those days, that line wasn't crossed. So she married a man her father had chosen, and that man—my great grandfather—had this chair hauled up to the attic the day it was delivered, because he knew it was from Tommy Buchanan."

She paused, remembering the family story that she had always cherished.

"But every day of her life, Great grandmother went up into the attic and sat in this chair, rocking . . . and thinking, I suppose, of how things might have been."

She frowned suddenly and looked up.

"I imagine that sounds like a very stupid story to you, and a very stupid reason to turn down a thousand dollars."

"What's your name?" he asked quietly.

"Molly."

"You were named after your great grandmother?"

Molly looked blankly at him. "How did you know her name? Was that in the catalog?"

"No," he said, dropping to his knees before the chair and bringing his eyes down to a level with hers. "He made two."

Molly leaned farther back, putting a little more distance between herself and this strange man who knelt at her feet.

"What are you talking about?"

"He made two chairs, absolutely identical." As if to prove his point, he reached under the left arm of the chair and, without looking, slid open the secret compartment that held the cracked sepia photograph. He pulled it out and smiled down at it a little ruefully. "He kept a photograph of Molly in his."

Molly's lips parted in surprise that anyone outside the family could know such things. "Are you a historian or something?"

"No," he chuckled, extending a hand calloused by labor. "Just another carpenter . . . and a great grandson. My name's Tom—Tom Buchanan—and the mate to this chair is in my living room."

Molly could only stare at him. She slipped her hand into his, feeling his strong fingers close around hers.

"When I read the auction notice for this house, I had this crazy idea"—he said, embarrassed—"that maybe after all this time, I could finally bring the two chairs together again."

He rose quickly to his feet and looked away, but not before Molly saw his cheeks flush a bright red.

She leaned back in the chair and started to rock slowly, smiling because she realized she'd been wrong all this time. Romantic souls still lived in these modern men with their modern clothes and cars and cell phones—you just had to look a little deeper. Or maybe, she thought, it was more than that. Maybe the two chairs had always been destined to bring two people together . . . if not at the time of their creation, then a century later.

She blushed at the foolish, fanciful path her thoughts had taken, then looked up at Tom Buchanan. Something about the way he smiled back at her made her wonder if he'd been thinking the very same thing.

"Would you like to see the other chair?" he asked her.

She automatically opened her mouth to politely refuse—she didn't know this man, after all—but then something hopeful rose within her, a trace of her great grandmother, perhaps, who had never been given the chance to say yes to her own Tommy Buchanan.

"Yes, I'd like that very much," Molly said, smiling up at him, absolutely certain that this was the way it was meant to be.

P. J. Platz

P. J. Platz is a pseudonym for the popular mother-daughter writing team of Traci and Patricia Lambrecht, today writing from Chisago City, Minnesota. Their prolific output includes eighteen novels, screenplays, poetry, and nearly a hundred short stories.

COME TO THE WEDDING

Jean S. O'Connell

It would be a wonderful wedding—after all, wasn't handsome, polished, and proper Ted going to be there too? Oh, she was so much in love with him! Perhaps he'd propose.

Instead, her boisterous, uninhibited, crazy family wrecked it all. She died inside seeing Ted, with that look of utter disbelief on his face.

And that Thatcher!

*G*randma arrived for the wedding wearing a beaded crepe de chine and carrying four knobbly brown-paper packages. The dress hung vaguely from the shoulders and was too long. Peering over the banister to watch Grandma's arrival, Lynn decided that she must have found the gown at a rummage sale. *Eccentrics,* Lynn thought unhappily, *this whole family is a bunch of eccentrics.* It was definitely a mistake, she knew now, to have Ted meet her family all at once like this. *I should have introduced him to them one at a time,* she thought. *Leaving Grandma for last.*

But it was too late for that now. She had been carried away with the idea of inviting Ted to be a house guest at this, her sister Alice's wedding, carried away with the idea of having him meet her whole large family en masse, at their best. Ted was to be an usher and Lynn the maid of honor. She had had no idea, when she had gone out with Ted all last winter and spring at college and fallen so in love with him, that he was an old childhood friend of the groom's. It was surely a miracle of fate.

She really wanted to make an impression. Ted Malone was a young man who thought family was important. He had said as much to her several times. And once he had taken her to his own, white-painted New England home. With Ted's mother, Lynn had looked at samplers and patchwork quilts that had been made by Malone forebears. When Ted's father showed her his garden, clipped and trimmed, she had thought of her own garden, which was usually full of other people's bicycles, galloping petunias, and her father, wearing shorts.

There was no doubt about it; Ted's family was really proper, and so was Ted. Once he had taken her to the Boston Symphony, and she had all but strangled, suppressing a cough. Afterward in his car, driving Lynn back to college, Ted had said, "It isn't just the music I love; it's the respect the people have for it. It's sort of holy at the symphony." And Lynn, wondering how many people had been strangling rather than listening, didn't say anything because she loved his "holy" remark. *He always saves himself from being stuffy,* she thought, *by some remark like that.*

"Where would you like to live, Ted, when you grow up?"

They were parked in front of Lynn's college dormitory, using up the last few minutes before the twelve-o'clock curfew.

He turned to her and laughed. "I've been grown-up ever since I can remember." His teeth were very even, and in the darkness his tanned face looked faintly Indian. "I'd live here, silly, near Boston." He paused. "You know, finish college next week, rest for the summer, go to work for Dunham and Evvarts in September." He said it as if he were reciting a creed.

It annoyed her. "And marry a nice New England girl," Lynn said, "and live happily ever after."

He leaned across the seat and kissed her full on the lips. "That's the only thing that isn't planned," he whispered. "Good night, Cinderella."

I love him, Lynn thought.

No one in Lynn's family had met Ted, and when she had suggested that he be a house guest, her mother had said, "Don't you think he'll think it's a little odd?" And Lynn had said, "There's nothing odd about being a house guest, Mother. After all, he is an usher. The only thing odd is this family." And after that her mother had said nothing more, nor had her father. Her brother Nathan had suggested that if this Ted person wore white, pointy-toed shoes like the last beau she had invited to visit, he was going to resign from the family; and her little brother,

Quintard, had asked if this Ted person would give him tips to go away, like the last one, whose name, he lovingly reminded Lynn, was Lester. She had kept her temper under control—and then Alice spoke up from her fog of bridal arrangements and said, "It's my wedding; all of you stop teasing her." So they all had. Ted had been invited and had arrived yesterday.

Lynn had walked to the station to meet him, thinking the stroll would be more romantic than a car trip. She had forgotten that he would be carrying a suitcase and that it might be a hot day. The stroll up from the station was punctuated only by grunts from Ted as he shifted the heavy suitcase from one hand to the other. And when Lynn said sentimentally, "This is where I played as a little girl," he said, "I wish you'd brought your bicycle along."

Halfway home they met Thatcher Jones. He was a friend of Nathan's, a neighbor, the boy who, often as not, took Lynn to the movies or played with Quintard to keep him out of trouble. Thatcher appeared from behind a bush, incongruously—but then, he was red-haired and freckled and skinny and kind of incongruous anyway.

"You must be Ted," Thatcher said, holding out his hand. "I'm the Singers' handyman." And he took Ted's suitcase before Lynn could say anything, and walked ahead of them up the sidewalk.

That Thatcher, Lynn thought. He was moving just a step ahead of them, so that, if they were not very careful, they would tread on his heels. And such heels. Huge grayish sneakers with holes in them covered Thatcher's sockless feet.

Thatcher turned his head and stared at Ted. "You aiming to marry this girl here?"

"Oh, shut up," Lynn said.

Ted looked at her sternly. To Thatcher he said, "Not today. It's too hot." They went the rest of the way to the house in silence.

There were two gigantic pine trees at one corner of the Singers' property, so it wasn't until they passed them and came abreast of the great, sprawling house that any of them saw the poster pasted to the pillar of the front porch.

It was a World War I poster, five feet high, with a lady painted on it, wearing a white garment. Underneath her floating feet was the legend, Give Till It Hurts.

Next to the poster, beaming proudly, stood Quintard, hair on end, barefoot. "It's so the guests will get the idea tomorrow," Quintard announced happily.

"I hope you brought a present, Ted Malone."

Thatcher sat down on the sidewalk and laughed hysterically.

Ted picked up the suitcase from where the hopelessly laughing Thatcher had dropped it, said, "I presume this is where you live," and marched into the house.

Since then, Lynn had guarded Ted from Quintard—and from Nathan, who, after all, had found the poster in the attic. She had made a tremendous effort to act decorous, hoping, willing the rest of the family to follow suit. So far, the only reaction had come from her mother, Miriam, who said, "Are you sick?" when Lynn had appeared for breakfast this morning, fully dressed and the first one up.

∎∎∎∎∎∎∎

Lynn looked again into the hallway below in time to see Thatcher step into the hall and take the packages from Grandma.

"What are you today?" Grandma asked. "One of Lynn's beaux or a disappointed lover of the bride?"

Thatcher grinned. His teeth stuck out a little, and it made his grin seem even more eager than he intended. "I'm on Lynn's side," he said. "I'm the old shoe."

And Lynn wondered quickly why Thatcher's remark didn't make her laugh. It made her feel suddenly a little sad. *That darn Thatcher,* she thought. *Him and his poetry.*

She watched Grandma climb the stairs with Thatcher behind her. Grandma was wearing black velvet pumps on her tiny feet instead of her usual sensible broad-toed shoes. As she rounded the last turn of the steps and smiled at Lynn, Lynn decided suddenly that the beaded crepe de chine was devastatingly becoming. *Why, she's impressive,* Lynn thought. *Like a sort of twinkling dowager.*

She took the bundles from Thatcher, who whistled. . . . She and Grandma went into the guest room.

Grandma said, "You ought to marry that Thatcher someday. He's our type. How's the bride?"

"Scared," Lynn said. *Our type indeed!*

Grandma smiled. "She shouldn't be. Harold is a nice boy. I like him. And heavens, they're so in love!"

I'm so in love, Lynn thought. For a moment, she forgot everything, thinking of herself and Ted getting married. Ted so handsome, so strong, so right. *I wonder,* she thought, *if Alice would lend me her cap and veil.*

"Wasn't there anyone," Lynn asked slowly, "out on the porch to help you bring those bundles in?"

"Some young man offered—an usher, I think—but I wouldn't let him."

"But you let Thatcher help you."

Grandma looked at her quickly. "How was I to know whether that usher was honest or not? Might make off with the family jewels." She drew forth from the brown-paper bundles her diamond bracelet and necklace and crescent pin, her sapphire rings, and a pair of diamond buckles for her shoes.

"Honest!" Lynn cried. "His forefathers came over on the *Mayflower!* Anyway," she added, "that's a crazy way to carry jewelry."

"I know," Grandma said. "I'm crazy." They looked at each other in the mirror. They had the same blue eyes, almond-shaped, the naturally curly hair of the Hughes family.

"Do you want me to approve of this young man?" Grandma asked. "Looked kind of stiff to me."

"He is not stiff—just well-bred," Lynn said, very loudly. "And his name is Ted Malone and I'd like to marry him. So there!" She turned abruptly, picked up her dress from the chair, and slipped it over her head.

"Oh, excuse me," Grandma said. She zipped the dress, then stood back for a minute, looking at the girl, at the thick auburn hair, the milk-white skin. "I had a blue dress with a hoop skirt once," she said. And then she turned and, with a most undowagerly gesture, hiked up the beaded crepe de chine, put her foot up on the bed and attached the buckles to her shoes.

Lynn laughed suddenly.

"How lovely you are," Grandma said. "Come, child; let's go and see the bride."

Alice was sitting in front of the dressing table in her room while her mother did something with pins and the shoulders of the wedding dress. In a twinkling, Grandma fixed the bothersome shoulder, and then she and Miriam together lifted the delicate lace-and-tulle veil from its stand and placed the cap on Alice's shiny gold head. Alice smiled her rare, gentle smile. *She is truly the most beautiful bride who ever lived,* Lynn thought. *I'm going to cry,* she thought, too, rather in a panic.

Lynn turned, left the room and went downstairs. *I have underestimated them all,* she thought sentimentally. *Today they will act like people of breeding—like Ted.* The house downstairs, swept bare of furniture, looked stately. Banks of flowers. Potted palms. Deliriously she thought, *Maybe today, in this setting, I shall become engaged.*

"Just like a wake," said Thatcher.

Lynn started, then ran from him out onto the front porch.

"Hello, beautiful," Ted said. "A New England girl could never be as lovely as you in that dress. I am struck dumb." He bowed from the waist. Quintard, standing next to him, bowed too.

Lynn began to feel slightly giddy.

Jonathan, Lynn's father, came out of the front door, looking festive, with a blue flower in his lapel. "Great day," he said.

Then up the long front walk came a man. In this small hiatus before the wedding, they all stood still and watched him. He approached the porch. "Mr. Singer?"

Lynn's father nodded.

"Didn't pay your telephone bill, sir, and we're going to have to discontinue service immediately if there's no payment. I'm sorry."

Mr. Singer reached into his pockets. Then he pulled his hands out again, turning the pockets inside out. "Cut it off," he said casually. "I'm broke. This suit's empty."

Lynn thought she had never seen a face as red as Ted's in her life before.

And then Thatcher's great, long, freckled hand, holding ten

dollars, reached out and tapped Mr. Singer on the shoulder. "You can have it without interest," Thatcher said.

Lynn looked around quickly. *He keeps materializing out of nowhere,* she thought. Thatcher was wearing a suit for once, she noticed, and a tie, and he looked like a neat, trim, redheaded beanpole. She began to forgive him for his remark about the wake.

Mr. Singer took the ten dollars and handed it to the telephone man. Then he turned to Quintard. "Go get that poster, son. Let's hang it right on the tree in the front lawn."

He looked then at Ted at just the same moment Lynn did, to see the look of shocked, disbelieving disapproval on his face. Mr. Singer smiled angelically. "It's only money."

Ted nodded. "I'm trying hard not to be sticky," he said.

And Mr. Singer and Thatcher laughed together like fools.

They're trying to act like eccentrics, Lynn thought hopelessly.

It was while Quintard was holding the poster up to the tree that Miriam appeared in the doorway. "Is everyone ready?" she asked.

And Mr. Singer bowed low and held out his hand to escort her onto the porch. Ted looked relieved that the situation had been saved; Thatcher stopped smirking; Nathan ran around the corner of the house and opened the door of one of the limousines and stood there at attention.

Hurray for Mother, Lynn thought, watching her go down the steps with her father, holding her long blue dress up carefully, every inch a lady, the mother of the bride.

"Quintard," Miriam said gently, when she came abreast of the tree, "do you know what I think of that poster?"

Quintard turned. "What, Mother?"

"I think it smells, dear," Miriam said. "Come now, get into the car."

I won't look at Ted, Lynn thought. *I can't stand it.*

Afterward, Lynn couldn't remember anything about the wedding except marching down the aisle with Ted when it was all over. Then she saw nothing, only Ted's profile. She didn't notice Thatcher, standing with her family, nor Grandma, next to him, only as tall as his shoulder; did not see that they wore identical, quizzical expressions as she and Ted marched by.

Lynn could not even count how many people said, "You'll be the next bride!" as she stood in the receiving line, nor how many people said, "Can it be Lynn, all grown up?" But she wondered, as she stood next to Alice, how much of it was true. That she was all grown up, she was quite sure. But the other—even walking down the aisle with her, Ted hadn't said a word, nor had he smiled.

Now she turned and looked toward him, in time to see Grandma introduce herself to Ted, smile her sudden, dazzling smile, and lead Ted to a table nearby.

Suddenly, Lynn had to know what they were saying, and so, when Thatcher came through the receiving line, she said, "My feet hurt," before he could even open his mouth, and led him to Grandma's table.

"Don't let us interrupt," Lynn said hastily.

"We only came to eavesdrop," Thatcher added. And Grandma laughed, but Lynn felt herself getting red in the face.

Ted sipped his drink slowly. "You're Mrs. Singer's mother?" he said to Grandma.

Grandma nodded. "My side of the family was European."

"The children have quite a sense of family," Ted said, then added, "Quintard, for instance. We were on the porch together this morning for a long time, and he talked about the family so much." He paused, awkwardly. "Its history," he added hesitantly.

"Was it about how his grandfather was found on a doorstep?" Grandma asked gently. She raised her glass. "It's entirely true," she said. "But they all knew his father was a prince." She drank. "And what's your family history?"

Ted cleared his throat. "I'm afraid mine isn't very cosmopolitan at all. You see, my ancestors came over on the Mayflower. Every generation of my family has lived in Boston since then."

"Puritans," Grandma said, and it was not a question.

Ted grinned. *"Touché."* Then he stood up. "Shall we dance?" he asked, and he and Grandma whirled away across the floor.

Lynn leaned forward abruptly, her face bright red. "Don't laugh," she said to Thatcher.

"I'm not laughing," Thatcher snapped. "I'm just feeling used. How come you didn't tell Ted that story? Usually you flaunt it around like a banner." When Lynn did not answer, Thatcher asked, "Do you want to dance now or do you want to sulk?"

He's jealous, Lynn thought, and wondered why it upset her so. But she stood up, and she and Thatcher danced together. She had forgotten how good he was. They whirled and dipped, showing off a little and loving it.

And then Ted cut in. Lynn hated herself for noticing immediately that Ted was not so good a dancer as Thatcher. Then she looked up at him and thought, *I've always been so crazy in love with him that I never noticed his dancing. I guess I'm always watching his face.*

But Ted's face wasn't looking down at hers. It was staring in a surprised way across the floor. Lynn turned her head.

Across the floor, Nathan was dancing with Grandma. They

made a touching picture. Why should Ted be surprised? Then she stopped dancing completely, as did everyone else. Because Nathan was teaching Grandma to jitterbug.

Grandma pirouetted neatly, and the diamond buckles flew off her shoes. Nathan retrieved them, and Grandma bowed a little and pinned them in her hair. The accordionist began to sing as he followed them about the room—*"Little old lady, sweet and shy."* Nathan, in a paroxysm of laughter, let Grandma dance alone. Grandma stood first on one foot, then the other, jiggling a little bit. Most of the guests were laughing—Ted was openly gawking. Lynn wondered if she would die of shame.

Then, as she danced by, Grandma reached out her hand. "Come, Lynn," Grandma said.

Firmly, she led Lynn through the big hallway and dining room, and then slipped with her through the kitchen door, swinging it back smartly in the accordionist's face. She led Lynn through the kitchen and out to a table set in the back yard near a clump of pine trees.

A waiter set a cup of coffee on the table, and Grandma sipped it gratefully. "I must be getting old," she said. She slipped the diamond buckles out of her hair and put them on the table. They twinkled in the late-afternoon sun.

Grandma sighed, then started removing her jewelry—the heavy necklace, the bracelet, the rings.

"Oh, put it on again, Grandma," Lynn said. "It makes you look so elegant."

And then Grandma's deep blue eyes became steely in color. Lynn could not look away. "I am not an elegant person," Grandma said. "But you'd like me to be, wouldn't you, Miss Lynn? You're actually sitting there thinking that I danced like that to humiliate you in front of that nice Ted boy who's so stiff."

"Well-bred," Lynn said weakly.

"Stiff," Grandma repeated. "Valiant, but stiff. Let me tell you something, little girl. I am dancing at this wedding because my eldest grandchild is marrying a nice young man. I am dancing because Miriam, my daughter, has always been so happy with Jonathan, your father, because I am proud of their fine, handsome family. I dance because this wedding is a symbol of many things for which I have always hoped for everyone in this home." She paused. "There are some people who would go to church under these circumstances," she said. "I thank God in my own way. I dance."

Lynn said nothing.

Grandma leaned forward a little. "Did you even see Alice kneeling at the altar? Did you notice the tears in your mother's eyes as she watched? Did you see Nathan as he stood up there, so handsome, watching his sister be married? Have you seen anything but yourself in that dress?"

Lynn sat still, blushing now.

Grandma pushed the diamond buckles across the table. "I wore these so I could give them to you today." Then she stood up, and Lynn felt like a child because Grandma was taller than she for a moment. "I remember a Lynn who would have danced with me," she added softly. Grandma kissed Lynn's head. "Forgive your old grandmother," she said. "I've missed you at the wedding, is all."

Lynn sat still as Grandma walked away, limping a little. And for a flashing second she knew that Grandma was right. But then her humiliation began to turn to anger. *She just doesn't understand that*

I've changed, is all. I've grown up, grown proper. I'm a woman in love; she ought to understand that.

She was sitting, still at the table where Grandma had left her. Just sitting there in her pretty blue dress, staring into the pine trees and not seeing them.

"You look as sour as an absinthe drinker," Thatcher's voice said. He sat down across from her, and as she watched his tall, thin form fold itself onto the small chair, Lynn had a sudden feeling of protection. She looked at him across the table, saw how his narrow shoulders were broadening out. She gazed at his face. Did his ears stick out less? She sat there, feeling a little frightened because suddenly Thatcher Jones was no longer the boy next door—he was a man, and it had all happened without her even noticing.

But she said, "Hi, Thatch," in her old bantering voice because it was a habit.

"What's the matter?"

She wanted now, suddenly, to confide in him, to rest her head on his shoulder and cry. "I seem to have missed the wedding," Lynn said in a wobbly voice. "Grandma says."

"Figure of speech, you mean."

Lynn nodded, unable to speak.

Thatcher fingered the diamond buckles that were still lying on the table. "These real?"

Lynn nodded. "My grandfather gave them to her."

"Must have loved her, all right," Thatcher said.

"Not necessarily."

Thatcher looked at her keenly. She could see the little laughter lines around his eyes clearly, because everything else was freckled. His long eyelashes were almost white from the sun. "Why should you say such a thing, Lynn?"

"If she knew about love, she'd understand," Lynn blurted. "Don't you think? Don't you think she'd know that love blinds you, that you get all wrapped up in yourself? That you just can't see anything else?"

Thatcher smiled a little. "Lynnie, I think if someone knew about love, they'd know it leaves you wide open."

"Not me," Lynn said, almost before she thought. "I mean, Grandma—all of them. Thatch, they ought to understand how important it is to me today that they all sort of—behave." *Oh, Lord,* she thought, *how can I explain my love for Ted? How can anyone understand?*

Thatcher sat back. "That's your problem," he said stiffly. And then he leaned forward. "It's a pretty big problem, you little fool. I'd have thought that by now you'd appreciate this whole big, lovely mob of a family you have. If you were me, you would. I have none. I think people who are ashamed of their families are just plain adolescent!"

He stood up, red in the face, and then he paused for a moment, looking at the girl. He looked for a long, long time, it seemed to Lynn. He pushed the diamond buckles across the table toward her.

"If I had a diamond," Thatcher said, "I'd give it to Grandma. For quality." He paused. "She give these to you?"

Lynn nodded.

"I can't imagine why," Thatcher said and walked away.

It was as if he had slapped her. Nothing had ever hurt her quite so much. Lynn picked up the diamond buckles and ran into the house, went through the kitchen, an incredible confusion of red-coated waiters, through the dining room, where remnants of wedding cake were everywhere, pushed her way through the hall, where people were singing, and finally arrived at the great, cool, quiet front porch. Here she could be alone.

The tears in her eyes kept her from seeing Ted until she was right next to him.

"Ah, there you are," Ted said. "I tried to find you, darling, but I've been surrounded."

"By my family, I suppose." Now that she was close to him, she found herself noticing that Thatcher was taller.

"Don't sound so resigned," Ted said. He reached out and pulled her toward him, held her in his good, firm arm. "Will you marry me?"

She leaned her head on his shoulder for a moment.

"Don't faint," Ted said. "Please."

"I won't." She pulled away from him a little, and went and sat on the wide porch railing and just looked at him. She looked at his handsome—oh, so handsome—face, at his perfect clothing. She looked at him and thought of his white New England home and his proper parents and his *Mayflower* ancestors. She thought of the magical nights she had danced with him at college; she thought of the dreams she had dreamed of becoming engaged to him. And she did not reply.

Ted sat down next to her. He took her hand and held it. "I know," he said—"what you're thinking. How different these families are. But, darling, it doesn't matter."

"I was thinking how noble it is of you to propose," Lynn said softly. Then she asked, "Why doesn't the family difference matter?"

"Because I don't plan to marry your family, Lynn. Just you."

"You mean you could go through another wedding—like this—just for me?" She spread her arms wide, as if to encompass the day.

Ted laughed. "I'd like it a little quieter."

But I wouldn't, Lynn thought suddenly. *I'd want it just as confusing and noisy and exhausting and touching. I'd want Grandma to dance, and Quintard to nail up posters . . . and Pop to forget to pay the telephone bill, because these are my people, my family. And I'd want Thatcher to—to what,* she wondered, and she knew what. She looked again at Ted.

"That would be impossible. My family would run the wedding."

"Not necessarily," Ted said. "I'd be the groom, after all."

No, Lynn thought. *Not at my wedding, you won't. Dear, dear Ted, I was so in love with you five minutes ago. Or was I just in love with myself?* Suddenly it seemed to her that she was being terribly unfair to Ted, that she had always been unfair to him. She started to cry.

"Ah, Lynn, don't do that." He hugged her. "We could wait. Two years or so. You'll be a lot more grown-up by then."

Lynn sniffed. "Oh, a lot more," she said. "But, darling, not grown-up enough to forget this whole family. I'll never be grown-up enough for that. You see, Ted, you're just not—our type."

Ted said, "You've been listening to too much propaganda."

"Maybe I have," she answered slowly. "Because I'm one of them. And when I'm an old lady, I'll dance at my granddaughter's wedding."

Ted sighed. "And your granddaughter will have red hair."

She looked at him quickly. "You really are grown-up."

"I told you that a long time ago, Lynn. One night at college."

She rested her head on his shoulder. "Forgive me for waiting until today to grow up myself," she said, and then she kissed him, deliberately and slowly and lovingly. Kissed him to say good-bye, kissed him to say thank you, kissed him because she had hurt him and hadn't meant to.

Ted held her off for a moment at arm's length. "You'll forgive me if I keep trying?" he asked.

"Of course." But she knew he wouldn't. She thought he sounded a little relieved.

Music blared from the house shrilly, suddenly, making them both jump. Nathan came out of the front door. "This you have to see," he said, half pushing them both toward the front hall.

Inside, within a circle of delighted spectators, squatted Johnny, the mailman, arms folded over his chest, doing a fast, insane kind of jumping dance to the accompaniment of the entire orchestra.

Thatcher yelled, "Come on, Lynn! He needs a partner!"

Johnny obligingly bounced himself over to one side of the circle to make room for her. She looked at Ted, thinking, *Never.* Then she looked again at Thatcher's grinning face, at Johnny's—he had taught her this dance during mail deliveries. And she reached into her pocket, took out the diamond buckles and attached them to her shoes. Then she folded her arms, squatted next to Johnny and danced like a dervish.

The diamond buckles twinkled as her feet moved. One flew off, and Thatcher retrieved it, and she pinned it in her hair. She was beginning to enjoy the wedding.

I DIDN'T EVEN
KNOW HER NUMBER

Arthur Milward

Young love does not necessarily begin in the mid-to-late teens. Sometimes it happens much earlier. What this true story reveals is this: The love of children can be so intense and so pure that nothing after it can really compare. Sometimes it lasts for a lifetime.

And sometimes . . .

She had long, shining black hair and the biggest brown eyes I had ever seen. She was, of course, very intelligent and played the piano like an angel (although I suppose that's really harps, isn't it?). Her name was Monika.

At nine years old, I happened to be between a tutor and a boarding school. My tutor (ex-tutor at this point, I suppose) had taken himself off to Austria on a mountain-climbing vacation, and the boarding school at which I had been reluctantly enrolled lacked three months until term time.

My parents, firm believers in unremitting industry—at least for me—had contrived to enroll me in a program for gifted children which convened in the city closest to our country home in Derbyshire, England. This would be marvelous for me, I was assured. I would get used to meeting and interacting with other children, and my brain would have no opportunity to go rusty in the interim period before I began to enjoy the inestimable advantages of the exclusive boarding school at which I had been enrolled before I was born.

I didn't say anything. For one thing no one was asking, and, by this stage in my life I was already a confirmed fatalist.

Actually, it was very different from my expectations. It was quite unlike what I imagined, in my total lack of experience, an ordinary school to be. The student body, contrary to the common practice, was comprised of both boys and girls, and the age range was wide, from about seven years old to one boy of fifteen.

My fellow students were, without exception, highly intelligent, and each had a specialty—almost an obsession, I observed—in which he or she excelled. The general curriculum, which everyone, including me, found not terribly challenging, was not taken too seriously by anyone and each of us spent most of his time engaging in the specialty of his choice.

There seemed to be plenty of teachers around. They were unobtrusive but were available to anyone who felt a need for advice, instruction, or who just wanted to chat.

The kids mostly worked alone—or in pairs—and there wasn't much of the interaction with which I had been threatened. I kind of liked the set-up.

I met Monika the second day I was there. For some reason she registered a day late and came in with her parents just as we were beginning work at about 9:30 in the morning. Her father paused and asked me, in German-accented English, as I happened to be near the door, whereabouts the music studios were located.

Her father and mother went into the office alone to sign papers and shell out money, I suppose, and Monika sat down near me to wait for them. She looked nervous, I thought, so, being a kind-hearted sort of kid, I engaged her in conversation and tried to put her at ease. Apart from which, I wanted to get a good look at her. I thought she was the most beautiful girl I had ever seen.

In addition to the aforementioned eyes and hair, I noticed that she had beautiful hands with long, slender, tapered fingers. She spoke softly, with what, to me, at any rate, was a delightful European accent. Always susceptible to beauty, I was immediately enchanted. School, I decided, was a great place, after all. Why hadn't I been afforded these marvelous experiences before? The inconceivable had taken place. My parents were absolutely right. With a heart overflowing with love and gratitude, I forgave them everything.

To cut a long story short, Monika and I quickly became inseparable. I listened to her play the piano (her specialty) and she read the poetry and prose I had been inspired to produce (my specialty). Some of the poems were even about her. She liked that and I liked her liking it.

What made things even better, my sainted parents had arranged lodgings for me in town for the duration of my stay at the school, and these lodgings (heaven was on my side; I began to say my prayers regularly again) happened to be just down the avenue from where Monika lived with her father, who was a research executive temporarily with the Rolls Royce Company, and her mother, who stayed home keeping things beautiful for her adored husband and only daughter.

The people with whom I was lodging had never had such an unobtrusive lodger. I spent most of my time when not in school at Monika's house. I would, of course, walk her home (somebody had to carry her music) and would invariably be urged to stay and eat and socialize for a while. I wasn't hard to persuade. I just called my lodgings to report my whereabouts and sort of took up residence.

Looking back, Herr Pickering, I suspect, regarded me with amused tolerance. His wife, however, made no secret of the fact that she thought I was wonderful. Having long held this opinion myself, I warmed to her immediately.

She would gaze at Monika and me, sitting on the step with our heads, one very blond, the other very dark, close together, engrossed in some activity or other and would make little clucking noises with her tongue. Sometimes her eyes would fill with tears, and she would come over and put her arms around the two of us.

I think she had some sort of a dream of our eventually rearing a line of progeny who would be sort of a cross between Shakespeare and Paderewski. Without having any clear idea of what it entailed, Monika and I thought this a marvelous idea and were eager to cooperate and ready for anything.

But it was not to be. As I said, I was already a fatalist. I guess I knew all along that the idyll couldn't last. Nothing ever had.

Just before the program closed for the end of the term, Monika's father was suddenly recalled by his parent firm in Hamburg, Germany. There was a lot of animated and sometimes tearful discussion in the household as to whether they should go or not. (The family was Jewish, and strange stories were filtering out of Europe about that time.) But in the end, disciplined, responsible Herr Pickering decided it was his duty to return with his family to his homeland.

Monika and I were heartbroken. We never got to celebrate her eleventh birthday together as we had planned. I don't suppose she ever received the little necklace I sent her for her birthday. We vowed to write, and I did. I got one letter.

The last news I had of Monika and her family came through another German family who had elected to remain in England. The Pickerings were last heard of in a place called Bergen-Belsen.★

I couldn't write to her there. I didn't even know her number.

★*One of the Nazi death camps. It was in this camp that Anne Frank died. Each prisoner had an identification number tatooed on their body (often on the arm). When I asked Mr. Milward about the last two lines of the story, he sighed and said, "I presume Monika died in that concentration camp, as no one ever heard of her again." That was Monika's last address.*

Arthur Milward

Arthur Milward was born in England and later emigrated to America. Besides his career in printing, he has a second—writing. a number of his true stories have been carried all over the world by *Reader's Digest*. Today, Mr. Milward lives and writes from Kennett Square, Pennsylvania.

YOUNG
MRS. RICHARD

Grace S. Richmond

Even if young Richard was his favorite grandson, Judge Richard Hazleton refused to admit the existence of Richard's violet-eyed bride, daughter of the judge's worst enemy. There didn't appear to be anything the young couple could do, for the judge was not one for changing directions once his course was set. But it was worth one more try.

*T*here are few people who can look unmoved at a bride on her wedding day. But Judge Richard Hazleton stood grimly by while his favorite grandson, Richard, was married to the girl of his choice, and nobody detected the least softening of his keen black eyes, or the slightest relaxation of the stern lines around his close-set mouth.

When congratulations became necessary, he marched slowly up to the young pair, standing flushed and smiling among the flowers, bowed stiffly to the new Mrs. Richard Hazleton, and looking coldly over her fair head, shook his grandson's hand without a word and turned away, a proud, unrelenting figure. Then he vanished from the house, and nobody saw him again that day.

"Never mind, dear," Richard whispered, "you'll win him yet."

She smiled back, with the least suspicion of wet lashes to intensify the beauty of her violet eyes. The look said, "I will," and Richard believed it and stood straight again, with a lift of the head singularly like that of Judge Hazleton himself.

For it mattered much what Grandfather Hazleton thought of Richard's marriage. The boy had lost both father and mother at an early age, and he and his brother Archer had been brought up by their paternal grandfather. Archer had finished his college course and gone away to the other side of the world several years before Richard had come to maturity. The younger brother had been Judge Hazleton's dearest treasure, whom he loved with a love as deep as it was reticent.

When, at twenty-six, Richard, on a successful footing of his own in the world, had announced to his grandfather his intention to marry the fair-haired girl with the eyes like blue violets, who had grown up in the big house next door and whose father was

Judge Hazleton's especial aversion, the old gentleman had been excessively displeased.

But he had not been able to advance a reason for his displeasure, beyond the insufficient one of his dislike to his neighbor and political rival, so the marriage had proceeded. For Richard, while loyal to his grandfather, was also loyal to the violet eyes and knew no just cause why any should forbid the banns.

Judge Hazleton himself did not forbid them, but he did all that he felt called upon to do in the matter when he went to the house of General Andrews during the brief period of the marriage ceremony.

"Grandfather," said Richard, coming in one morning when he and Evelyn had returned from their wedding trip and had taken up a temporary abode next door, "we've decided on a house—if we can get it. Will you sell us one of yours?"

His tone was precisely as if nothing unusual had happened. The judge eyed him severely over his gold-bowed spectacles.

"Which one? The Singleton place, I suppose."

"No, sir. Aunt Martha's old house on Albemarle Street."

The judge took off his glasses and wiped them. "May I inquire why you have selected that?"

"It is within my means—I hope," explained Richard, promptly. "The Singleton place is not. We don't care to start off with a pretense of style beyond our income. Besides, Evelyn prefers the old house."

Judge Hazleton grunted—it could be called nothing else. Then he replaced his spectacles, took up his pen, and went on with the writing Richard had interrupted. The young man waited silently, but with a peculiar curve at the corners of his mouth. He had not lived for twenty years with the head of the State Supreme Court without learning that there is a time for the withholding of speech.

The old gentleman finished his page, blotted it, and said without looking up:

"I will rent the house to you. I do not wish to sell it. It would not be worth your while to buy it. Your bird will demand a cage with more gilding before very long. She's too young to know her own mind yet."

His grandson's eyes sparkled with the quick retort which he did not allow to reach his lips. He rose with a quiet, "Very well, sir; thank you," and left the room.

Outside on the street he rejoined his young wife with a smothered whoop of delight. "We can rent it!" he told her gleefully. "I did not dare expect as much as that."

"I hoped he would be pleased that we wanted it," she said with a shadow of disappointment in her eyes.

"Don't you flatter yourself he'd show it. Not he. That'll come later, when we've carried out your little schemes. That is—I hope it will. It will take a long storming of the citadel and a tremendous battering of the fortifications to carry off the enemy into our country. But we'll do it. He shall own some day that my wife—"

He finished the sentence with a look more eloquent than the words he could not find. Then the two walked over to Albemarle Street, to go by the quaint little house with the green blinds, where Evelyn had chosen to live chiefly that she might win Grandfather Hazleton's heart into her keeping.

Putting the place in order took two months. All Richard's spare time was given to the ransacking of the shops, and of certain other places, with Evelyn, for suitable furnishing for the new home. This differed greatly from the ordinary shopping of the newly wedded, the fashion whereof shall be told later.

On a bleak day in December the two, having begun house-keeping, separated at the door of the house on Albemarle Street with a somewhat singular conversation. Evelyn was anxiously scanning the heavens—especially in the northeast.

"Don't you think it is sure to storm, Richard?" she asked. "The papers certainly say so."

"It surely will, dear. Look at that blackness in the east now."

"Oh, I hope so! If it will only be a real 'nor'easter,' one that will last a day or two—with his rheumatism! But, Richard, it may begin before you get him here. Do hurry!"

Richard ran down the steps laughing, and waved his hat back at her from the bottom.

"Here's to our desperate schemes, little plotter!" he cried softly. "May a great storm come up out of the North Atlantic seas and blow into Grandfather Hazleton a fervent appreciation of the blink of our ain fireside. I'll bring him back with me, Evelyn, if it can be done. Meanwhile don't let the duck burn up!"

He hurried away, and presently Judge Hazleton, sitting gloom-ily in his library, nursing a left leg which already felt the oncom-ing storm, heard himself addressed by the familiar cheery voice. He had missed that voice and felt an ache which he would not own, but which hurt nonetheless for that.

"Many happy returns, Grandfather!" cried Richard, and Rich-ard's handsome face beamed at him from the doorway.

"Come in," said the judge. He said it without much relaxation of countenance, to be sure, but with a milder inflection than he had employed toward his grandson of late.

The young man came in gaily, bringing an atmosphere of fresh air and youth and health with him, as he had ever done. He sat down on the arm of a big chair, opposite his grandfather. He had not removed his overcoat; his hat was in his hand.

"It's a cold day," he said, "but the air is fine, and a breath of it would do you good. Let me order the horses, will you, sir, and come over to Albemarle Street with me? There's a little birthday dinner waiting for you there, a magnificent old fireplace in Aunt Martha's house—remember it, sir?—and the jolliest fire is roaring up the chimney this minute. Please, Grandfather!"

The old man hesitated. Rejection was in his eye, refusal on his lips, but it was a little difficult to meet with his customary curt "no" an invitation like this, bubbling over with goodwill and heartiness. Meanwhile Richard came lightly across the floor and dropped upon one knee before Judge Richard Hazleton. He laid one warm hand on the judge's cold one, looked up, laughing, and sued for the favor.

"Please, sir!" he said. "It's your birthday. You never denied me a favor on your birthday, Grandfather."

The judge stirred uneasily, moistened his lips, got slowly and stiffly to his feet, and reached for his cane.

"Well, well, boy," he said gruffly, "this once! But not again, mind you."

Now Grandfather Hazleton had not addressed one word to Richard's wife since the wedding day—and you will remember that he had not addressed her then. So it might easily have been an embarrassing moment all around when the Hazleton coachman drew up before Aunt Martha's old house in Albemarle Street, and Evelyn appeared at the top of the steps to greet the two coming up them by painful stages.

The black clouds in the northeast were gathering thickly, and the judge's rheumatism was growing very bad indeed. But Richard looked up confidently with a cheerful "Here we are!" and the blithest voice in the world responded, "I'm so glad! Come in out of this wretched cold to our splendid fire!" And somehow there was no greeting necessary.

Judge Hazleton did not offer to shake hands with young Mrs. Richard, but nobody appeared to notice that, and the two had him out of his overcoat and into a big easy chair in front of the fire before he had time to object or to know what he was about.

They did not try to make him talk. Richard was all about the room, saying gay things first from this corner, then from that. Evelyn flitted in and out, half-covered by a big white apron with a most fetching ruffled bib.

Savory odors floated in each time she opened the dining-room door, and the judge's nostrils detected the delicious fragrance of—was it roast duck? There was a suspicion of spiciness in the air, too, which might or might not be that of mince pies. The judge especially liked mince pies.

There were a few moments when Evelyn called Richard out to assist her with something. Then the judge sat up straight in his chair, turned and glanced sharply about the room.

His first impression, then, had been correct. Instead of being furnished in the latest modern style, the long, low-ceiled apartment was a veritable reproduction of the best of oldtime living rooms.

A quaint, flowered paper covered the walls; fine pieces of old mahogany stood here and there; a slender-legged table that he could have sworn belonged to his mother was at his elbow. Bits of old china caught his eye upon the chimneypiece; over it hung—yes, actually—a long discarded but undeniably fine portrait of the judge himself in his youthful days.

He heard them coming laughing back and sank into his chair again, his lips setting tightly. His eyes fixed themselves on the fire, and Richard had to say twice, "Grandfather, our little dinner is served. Will you come out, sir?" before the guest pulled himself together and, with the necessary aid of his grandson's arm, limped slowly out.

What a dinner! And such a table—for that was what first demanded the grudging attention of the guest.

Surely he recognized those thin, white plates and cups and saucers with the delicate green sprigs. Absently his finger touched one of the sprigs on his plate. As a boy at his mother's table he had always been impelled to feel of them to see if they would push off. They would not push off any more readily now than they would then. He drew away his finger, and his eyes traveled to the walls of the room, and he started slightly in his chair.

"Do you recognize Grandmother's old sideboard?" asked Richard, slicing off thin morsels of rich and tender duck with quite a skillful hand for one so new at carving—and everybody knows that ducks are hard carving, too. "And this is her dinner set. Aunt Patience let us have all these things when she found that we really cared—that Evelyn cared. We do care, sir; and Evelyn more than I. It's all her idea. I suppose I should naturally have started in with a new house and new furniture—varnish not dry, you know—patent oak rockers and green marble center tables, and cheap etchings on the wall—"

"Richard!" How pretty her face was, flushed and laughing in protest, in the soft light from the candles! Richard gave her an answering glance, full of fun and mischief—but with his heart in it, nonetheless.

"He loves the dear old things just as well as I do!" Evelyn declared, pouring coffee and putting in a generous supply of rich cream.

Then she held the old-fashioned sugar tongs poised above the green-and-white sugar bowl. She looked up full into Judge Hazleton's face with a daring pair of violet eyes.

"How many lumps, Grandfather?" she asked, and flushed a rosier red than ever. But her glance did not flinch.

In the short pause that followed, Richard dared not look up; he kept his eyes fixed on the centerpiece. But he listened, with his heart in his mouth. Question and answer had not yet passed between the two.

"Two," said Judge Hazleton, and his black eyes went for an instant deep into the violet ones, with a searching power which made his grandson feel as if he would like to jump between.

But Evelyn met him with a frank smile, dropped in the two lumps, and gave him the cup. Richard drew a long breath.

The dinner was superb. Where it came from or who cooked it Judge Hazleton did not know, but it suited his critical taste. It ended with an old-fashioned plum pudding. Comment the guest made none, but he swallowed his share of the pudding to the last crumb. Richard smiled to himself as he noted the fact.

"Jove, but the wind blows!" said the young host, as they came back to the fire in the front room. "Hear the windows rattle!"

He raised the curtain and looked out. "It's storming furiously!" he cried. "And by all that's great, Grandfather, I believe I didn't tell Michael to come for you!"

"Telephone," said the judge.

"Why, we haven't had one put in yet. Too bad! Of course I can go out and send word from somewhere. But—suppose you don't go out, Grandfather? You know such a storm is pretty hard on your rheumatism."

"I must go home tonight!" said the judge, as sternly as if much depended on his return.

He got up and made his way to the front door and opened it.

A tremendous blast threw the heavy oak back upon him, knocked his spectacles from his nose, and cut him through with its penetrating chill.

He drew back, his heavy white hair erect and dancing in a most undignified way, and Richard, throwing his weight against the door, closed it. Evelyn picked up the spectacles. The judge limped back without a word. The two behind him glanced at one another triumphantly.

"Sing for us, dear," proposed Richard. "Perhaps the worst of the storm will be over presently."

The girl went over to the piano; it was the only modern thing in the room. She played softly and sang in a clear, young contralto voice which had in it a quality of the sort which touches heartstrings. She sang modern songs at first, Grieg and Nevin and Chaminade. But presently she gave them "Annie Laurie."

Then the judge got suddenly up. "If I must stay," he said, abruptly, "I think I will go to bed."

Evelyn lit a candle, and Richard offered his arm again up the short staircase. The judge climbed slowly, breathing somewhat heavily. Richard led him to the front room and stopped with his hand on the latch.

"We furnished this room, sir," he said, in his clear voice, which nevertheless shook a little, "just for you. We hoped you might like to stay here with us sometimes, and feel that it was home. Aunt Patience sent for most of the things. They came from the old place up in New Hampshire, and she says they are the ones you and Grandmother had when you kept house—when Father was a boy. We hope you'll like it, sir. You don't know how much we want to please you, Grandfather—Evelyn and I."

He opened the door, and the judge walked in—much as if he would have preferred to stay outside. A small fire crackling cheerily in the odd little fireplace threw its wavering light on the quaint blue-and-white "landscape" paper which covered the walls.

A four-poster bed, hung with dimity, was there, a shining high mahogany chest of drawers, a little washstand with a blue-and-white pitcher and bowl. High-backed chairs stood about, with one cozily cushioned big rocker in front of the fire; on the floor lay the prettiest of old Turkey carpets.

Grandfather Hazleton looked about with dazed eyes. They all stood silent for a moment; then a gentle hand fell on his arm, and he stared down for the second time that evening into a well-nigh irresistible pair of eyes.

"It's been such a happiness to get it ready for you!" said the voice to which Richard had long sworn allegiance. "Won't you forgive us for loving each other and for not being content without your approval and your—love?"

It was a long moment, and again his grandson held his breath, feeling that if the elder man spurned the girl now, he, Richard, must henceforth refuse to be to him that which he had been all his life.

But there is a temperature at which the hardest substances melt, and perhaps it was not Judge Hazleton's heart which was at fault, after all, only his pride; and pride cannot endure before love. Suddenly he turned and laid both hands upon Evelyn's shoulders, bent, and kissed her gently on the forehead. Then he went over to the fire and sat down.

Richard, with a radiant face, let Evelyn draw him quietly away out into the hall and noiselessly closed the door. Then he triumphed openly.

"You've done it, little girl, you've done it, bless you!" he whispered.

They went silently and joyfully downstairs. But they did not know that in the little bedroom, which looked like the home of his youth, an old man sat and wiped away the tears—tears which meant things the younger people, with all their love and good-will, could never understand.

Grace S. Richmond
(1866–1959)

Grace S. Richmond of Fredonia, New York, was known as "The Novelist of the Home" and was one of the best-known writers of novels and short stories in America, remembered most, perhaps, for best-sellers such as *The Twenty-Fourth of June, Red Pepper Burns, Red and Black,* and *Foursquare.*

THE TROUBLE
WITH ARABELLA

Robert Bassing

*P*aul *had always had an insidious ability to bring on what the locals euphemistically called "Arabella's trouble." Once he moved away, she outgrew it.*

Well, now she was grown-up, beautiful, engaged, and he was here for her marriage to Junior Gould. And Paul would most likely marry fashion model Nance Tinderly. But before that could happen, there was a wedding service to get through.

*W*hen we were in school together, I never took Arabella Badmington very seriously, for the simple reason that she didn't fit in with my plans. She was a nice kid, sweet and pretty, in a starched-dress sort of way. But I had already picked out the girl I wanted.

I had found her one day in a magazine in a full-page travel advertisement for the Bahamas. She was tall and chic, and in a splash of festive Technicolored photographs, she was posed decoratively at the side of her handsome, evening-coated, bathing-suited, hunting-jacketed escort (me, that is). She was an ultra sophisticated young thing who fitted in perfectly with my plans. She turned out, years later, to be Nance Tinderly.

When, after I met her in Chicago, Nance and I first began to see each other as a steady arrangement, I marveled at my good fortune. But as time went on, the enchantment began to slip away from our romance, like a slow leak in a tire. It reached an all-time low one warm, spring midnight when I was driving Nance home in my convertible along the lake shore. We had just come from a gigantic bore of a dinner at twenty-five dollars a plate.

"Why?" I asked, turning to look at her, relaxed comfortably beside me. She had been beautiful all evening, in a new gown, slim and chic, her blond hair brushed soft and then tied severely back. "What's the big attraction in showing off around these people? They're out of our element. I don't know what to talk to them about. They wouldn't understand me if I did."

Nance laughed and reached over to the wheel and patted my hand. "I know you didn't have a good time tonight," she said. "And I suppose if I were going to analyze it, I didn't either. But I enjoyed being there. I knew I looked smart and you were very handsome and we made an impressive couple. I liked being younger than the others. You didn't notice it but they beamed on us."

"So what? If you didn't have a good time?"

"Well, I did, in a way. It's what I'm trying to tell you. You have to learn, as I have, to play a game, darling. Whenever you go out, you play a game. You pretend that you are very exquisitely beautiful and successful and that everyone is impressed with you and wants to take you up. First thing you know, it comes true."

"And then what? What do you pretend then?"

"Once you know how to play the game, there's no end to the things you can pretend." Nance laughed. "I've just told you a very personal secret. You mustn't ever tell."

I was confused. I was in a foul mood, and the best thing was to get Nance home as quickly as possible before I said what was on my mind.

It has been said that the Lord works in mysterious ways, and if that was true, then it would follow with perfect reason that he would get my kid sister Janice to help him. There was a letter from her waiting for me when I got home that night. She couldn't have timed it better.

"When are you going to take a day off and come home and see us?" she wrote. "Don't you remember Connecticut in the spring? What are you doing way out there when it's spring here in Mystic? I have bad news for you, old man. I guess you're going to die a bachelor. And don't say I didn't warn you. Arabella Badmington is engaged to Junior Gould! You heard me the first time. And what did you expect? Did you think she'd wait forever? I guess the years of heartbreak dampened her spirit. Incidentally, her 'trouble' has disappeared, died on the vine along with her heart while you've been making it big in Chicago.

Well, you've lost out, and, poor me, I've lost out too. Lost the nicest sister-in-law a girl ever knocked herself out to have."

Janice was being funny. If there had ever been anything romantic between Arabella Badmington and me, it was created by Janice's imagination. I was reminded of this in her first letters after I left home. "Won't you send at least a postcard to your poor Arabella? Don't you know the child is pining?" I always meant to get off a letter to Arabella but I never made it.

I had been in Chicago a year when Janice, who had remained at home with our Aunt Hattie, announced her engagement to Jack Stanley. "And you've got to come home," she wrote, "and give the child bride away. After all, a girl of nineteen is altogether too young to give herself up to a man! At least, that's what Aunt Hattie keeps telling me. I need you here anyway to handle her. That one! She and her Old Folansbee will be the death of me. Incidentally, Arabella's my bridesmaid. What do you say you two get married at the same time? Say yes. I think the poor girl's going to feel like an old maid unless somebody rescues her."

Arabella was nineteen too. And when I went back for the wedding, she was just the way she had been the year before, a quiet, bright-eyed child who never escaped from looking as if her mother had sent her out of the house in a clean starched dress and told her not to get dirty.

Despite the fact that Arabella was not the chic and sophisticated enchantress of my dreams, she did hold one strong fascination for me. I learned a secret about her early, when we were all kids: I could make her laugh. I never missed an opportunity to torment her because of it. Somewhere deep down under the starch and the pale, freckled propriety, a perverse part of Arabella found life intolerably funny. It had been the most curious, most delightful sensation for me to come upon this. It was as if I had picked up a glass of water and found it bubbling with champagne. Because of it, I nearly ruined Arabella's reputation in Mystic. She developed what everybody began to refer to as "Arabella's trouble."

For example, I remember Aunt Hattie's sixtieth birthday party. There were maybe fifty of us crowded into our two front rooms, all getting silly on nonalcoholic punch, and Old Folansbee, whose middle had outgrown his only good suit, stood up to make a speech. He made terrible speeches, but everybody put up with them—for old times' sake, I guess. It was general knowledge that he and Aunt Hattie had been engaged in what was probably the stormiest courtship in Connecticut history and unquestionably the longest, since it was going on before most of us were born. When they were in harmony, they dated for church every Sunday and spent several evenings a week helping each other piece together super-jumbo jigsaw puzzles. And then they would not be speaking to each other because one night they would have quarreled, and for weeks at a time they would wrangle and finally patch it up.

It was always at such a function as Aunt Hattie's birthday party that this thing would happen to Arabella, and I was always the one who brought it on. I became so talented at it that I knew instinctively the right moment, and I would half-close my eyes and stare at her in a certain way, and then, always, the look of despair would come over Arabella's face and it would begin to happen.

Old Folansbee squeezed his hands into his pockets and began to sway back and forth with his eyes closed, winding up for a lengthy salute to Aunt Hattie's sixty years. She was sitting stiffly, corseted into a new pink dress, with a bright pink flush on her face and a pink corsage pinned to her shoulder and her hair in springy yellow-white curls. Everyone was smiling pleasantly except Arabella, who, with hands folded in her lap, was sitting on the sofa across from Old Folansbee, staring down at the carpet. She was wearing a blue-and-white striped dress and white socks. Her black hair was braided in two pigtails, and the only makeup she wore was a straight line of pale pink lipstick.

I found a place against the wall, just out of Folansbee's line of vision, and I leaned there with my hands in my pockets and stared at Arabella, waiting.

Folansbee had lost the subject for the fourth time, off on some tangent about the city's fireplugs, when Arabella sighed and glanced up and saw me. I didn't move. I just stared at her. Quickly she looked down at the carpet, and in a moment I began to detect the first signs. She was biting her lips and taking deeper breaths. She raised her head again, and ruthlessly I ignored the plea for mercy on her face. I half-closed my eyes and stared at her in that special way. And it began to happen. I watched, fascinated at what I had wrought, as she sucked in her cheeks and bit them and held her breath. Then, to hasten her along the path to destruction, I nod-ded, indicating Old Folansbee's foot, which was doing a nervous little toe dance, and when Arabella saw that, she let out her breath in a terrible, explosive burst—"Ppppfffft!" and screamed.

It was like setting off a firecracker at a meeting of the Ladies' Aid. Folansbee choked and whirled around and glared at her. Aunt Hattie's pink face turned red and a high-pitched squeal of outrage burst from her puckered mouth. Everybody else began to mutter that Arabella had done it again and then they fell silent and stared at her, waiting for her to stop laughing or at least to excuse herself from the room. The picture of them all staring at her as if she were not right in the head struck her as so funny that she shrieked again and clamped her hand over her mouth and then fell back onto the sofa in a fit of laughter.

Finally I went over and got Arabella by the arm and pulled her, stumbling, out of the parlor and down the front walk to the maple tree. We fell against it, laughing until we thought we would die, and we stayed there until everyone came out onto the porch for supper and it would be safe in case we got going again.

The morning after I got Janice's letter inviting me home for a visit to Mystic, I invented an excuse to tell my office, which was the sort of thing I hadn't done in years, and then I telephoned Nance and told her the same shameful excuse, that my Aunt Hattie was ill and that I had to rush home.

In an hour I was out of the city. I was actually going home, going to see Janice again and Mystic in the spring. I was alone in the car and felt, all at once, very young and unattached. I began to whistle a Sousa march.

I had played third clarinet in the school band, which meant that I picked up the rear of a group of eight clarinetists and sometimes got to bleat a note or two. I would have turned in my instrument had it not been for the fact that band practice afforded me a reserved front-row seat in the band pit for the weekly assemblies in the school auditorium where I could watch either the stage or the audience. From this vantage point I found a release from the frustration of my back-seat performance by making the weekly assemblies the scourge of Arabella Badmington's life.

One of my greatest triumphs materialized the day a missionary from one of the South Sea islands visited the school and recited the Lord's Prayer in native sign language. He was a heavy man who wore a black suit cut full to fit over his large, unwieldy hips. Preliminary to his demonstration, he described the beauty of the prayer as the islanders pantomimed it, and if he had been a slim and graceful native girl, I guess the act would have lived up to his promise. Tension in the auditorium increased by the second, and in the awful silence you could hear only the missionary's breathing.

When he opened his mouth and began to push his fingers into it, showing "our daily bread," I knew what I had to do and nothing could have stopped me. I searched through the rows of students until I found Arabella. She was looking down at the floor, and she had turned very pale. I stared at her steadily until she saw me, and then I half-closed my eyes and let her have it. It was a matter of seconds before she began to hold her breath, her face flushed in panic. The squeal which finally burst from her throat wasn't terribly loud, but in the awful stillness of the auditorium you could have heard a fly cough. Students turned in their seats and some of the girls began to giggle, and then Arabella was lost, sinking, drowning in laughter. In a moment, the auditorium was in bedlam, everybody screaming uncontrollably.

It was after that assembly that they arranged an interview for Arabella with the psychologist from the board of education, who tried to determine what was behind her "antisocial" outbursts. She gave Arabella a helpful book, and Arabella studied it for days, trying desperately to uncover the secret to self-control.

On Sunday afternoon, three days after I left Chicago, I turned the convertible onto the narrow, tree-shaded New England street and pulled up in front of the family home. Fortunately, I had sent Janice a wire the day before, so my arrival was not a surprise to them. The only thing was, I had walked into a garden party Janice had previously planned for Arabella and Junior Gould.

"See," Janice said, after I hugged her and then held her at arm's length so that I could get a look at her. "I whipped you up a party at a moment's notice."

I liked the way she looked, small and all golden in a yellow dress and the same, exactly the same, wise pixy face.

"If you're satisfied with my appearance," she said, "you'd better come say hello to everybody, beginning with Aunt Hattie. She's decided you've had an automobile accident." She took me by the hand and led me up the walk through the crepe paper arbors, chattering. "Jack's gone out for ice cream with Junior Gould. They'll be right back."

Neither Aunt Hattie nor Old Folansbee had aged a minute. They were sitting together in wicker chairs on the porch, absorbed in whatever dialogue had been fascinating them for the last thirty years.

"Did Janice tell you, Paul," Aunt Hattie said, after she had given me two of her dry, powdery kisses, "that I thought you had an automobile accident?"

"Yes, Aunt Hattie, I told him," Janice informed her.

"It was only a small one," I said. "They took eighteen stitches, gave me a pint of blood, and I was back on the road in an hour."

Janice said, "He's teasing you, dear."

Aunt Hattie looked hurt. "Oh, Paul, you're teasing me! You didn't have an accident."

"Sorry, Aunt Hattie. Next time."

"Put on a little weight, young fellow," Folansbee said.

"Maturing," I said. "Always maturing."

Suddenly, Janice remembered that she had left Arabella in the kitchen cutting cake. "When you arrived, I forgot about her!"

she exclaimed. She grabbed my arm, and we went racing around to the back door and into the kitchen.

"You poor little thing!" Janice shouted. "I forgot all about you and this is your party. Anyway, I brought you a surprise. Look."

The surprise was supposed to be me. But, as it turned out, the surprise was on me. I don't mean to say that Arabella was a ravishing beauty. But she wasn't wearing a starched dress and her lipstick wasn't a straight pink line. She—well, she had grown up. And she was lovely.

"Hello, Paul," she said and held out her hand.

"Shake the girl's hand," Janice said. "And then kick yourself. You're too late, you dope."

I took her hand. "It's awfully good to see you, Arabella."

"It's awfully good to see you."

"It's awfully good if it doesn't rain," Janice said.

"Why don't you . . . go and polish a few guests," I said to Janice. "And I'll help out here."

"I thought you would," Janice said. "The boys ought to be back any minute with the ice cream, and then we've got to get everybody together. Old Folansbee has a few million words to say." She stood at the door to the dining room. "Paul?"

"What?"

"Remember. She's engaged." The door closed after her.

"You know," I said, "I'd almost forgotten how much I hate her."

Arabella laughed, a polite, easy laugh.

"Let me look at you," I said. She turned and faced me. "I don't feel I know you. You've changed . . . a great deal."

"No, I haven't. Janice makes me out to sound like the ugly duckling transformed into a swan. And I'm not."

"But you are."

She smiled and picked up a knife and began to cut a huge loaf cake into squares. "Here, Paul, fix these on that platter . . ."

In some ways, she reminded me of Nance. Partly, it was the way she had her hair brushed up softly, and it was because she had Nance's slimness and same easy posture. But there was something else. She had poise, the last thing I would have expected to see in Arabella.

"How's your 'trouble'?" I asked.

"My trouble," she said, "disappeared when *you* did. Folks marveled at the change in me."

"You really can't blame me. You were a silly kid."

"I used to wonder what was ever going to become of me. I remember being terribly, secretly relieved when you left." She handed me a piece of cake. I put it on the platter. "And, by the way, I'm cross with you. I wrote you three letters after you left, and you never answered one of them."

"I meant to. I'm just not the writing type. Is that what sobered your spirit?"

"Broke my heart." She smiled. "I'll tell you a secret. I had an awful crush on you and you never knew it."

I felt embarrassed and for some strange reason my heart began to pound very hard. "I wish I'd known. All I knew was I liked to make you laugh."

"I suppose you thought there was something wrong with me too."

"Not at all. I thought you were intelligently appreciative of my supreme wit. What happened to your crush?"

"I outgrew it."

"Don't you feel anything now . . . talking to me?"

Arabella smiled slowly. "You know, you're flirting with me."

"I didn't know."

"And I'm practically married."

"But not quite."

"A week away."

"A week!" I shouted. "I thought it was months away."

"No. Next Sunday. You'll be here for the wedding."

"I . . . may have to leave before. Anyway, what's the big rush?"

"There's no rush," she said. "We've been going together for a long time. I work with Hank in the store. Hank manages the hardware. His father manages notions. And I'm bookkeeper. That's how we got to know each other."

"You're in love with him?"

"That's a funny thing to ask," she said. "Why would I be marrying him?"

"I don't know. I don't even remember him very well. I don't know why I asked."

The back door opened and Junior Gould came in, loaded down with ice cream, and went for the sinkboard.

"We got more ginger ale too," Junior said.

I remembered him immediately, not so much as he had been when I knew him in school, but because I remembered his father and because Junior was one of those people who had matured into a remarkably accurate reproduction of his parent. He was stocky, a few inches taller than Arabella, and his neck, just like his father's, was the same girth as his head and it seemed to contain all of his personality. His voice was deep and tightly constricted within the rigidity of his neck. When we were kids, Janice and I used to do imitations of Hank, Sr., pulling in our chins and struggling, as Hank always did, to get free of our collars. It seemed to me now that Arabella used to be in on these games, too, but she would have forgotten.

"Hello, Junior," I said.

He turned from the sinkboard, where he had put the ice cream, and struggled for a moment, setting his collar straight.

"Paul! Well, what do you know! How's it been treating you?"

We shook hands . . . ruggedly. "It's been treating me OK. I don't have to ask how it's treating you," I said, indicating Arabella. "You must be on top of the world."

"That's what they tell me," Junior said, feigning modesty. "All I know is, she's really got me hooked. That right, Bella?"

"Somebody open this door for me!" It was my brother-in-law, Jack Stanley, with a case of ginger ale.

"Hold on," I said and went to the door.

"Oh, it's *you*," Jack said. "Well, how you been, Paul? Quite a surprise, you coming home for the wedding."

Jack was a nice guy, with only one drawback, as far as I was concerned. At some point in his education, he had acquired a prejudice against brothers-in-law. To him, they were all people in jokes who hit you for a loan, lived in your spare room and used up all your shaving cream. He was wary of me. Wouldn't trust me to walk across the street and buy him a paper. Also, he was Junior Gould's best friend.

"I didn't exactly come home for the wedding," I said. "I came to see you about a little business matter."

"Oh?" he said, looking trapped.

Janice pushed open the dining-room door. "You're all here. Good. We've got to get everybody into the parlor for Folansbee's speech before the ice cream melts."

It was like old times, all of us crowded in there. I settled back against the doorjamb listening to Old Folansbee. I watched Arabella seated between Aunt Hattie and Junior Gould. She sat on the edge of the sofa, erect, with her hands folded comfortably in her lap.

"Now, young love," Folansbee was saying, "is one of the two things this modern world ain't changed. The other thing is Sundays." Everybody laughed, because he looked over his spectacles and waited. "They can bring their hydrogen bombs and frozen vegetables and speed up the pace of living, but they can't change Sundays. I guess God sees to that."

He went on to talk about Sundays, and Arabella looked over at me and smiled. I couldn't help it, I had to see. I half-closed my eyes and looked at her steadily, in that old way. Once, it would have been the end of Folansbee's speech. Arabella winked at me and returned her attention to Folansbee.

"And young love," he resumed, "is the other thing God's watching out for. It's a good thing too. Because, I guess if he wasn't, we'd all be going to the market and picking up a package of it at the frozen-food counter." Everybody chuckled and looked at one another knowingly. Arabella laughed politely. Junior Gould held his chin in close to his collar and laughed self-consciously, "Ho, ho, ho," as if Folansbee were telling a story on him.

Everybody was very happy. But I felt lost and alien. I knew when Arabella winked at me that she had outgrown her trouble and that a part of me was gone. I longed to be back with Nance.

There was no reason now to hang around Mystic, except that I couldn't be rude to Janice and I felt committed to stay for Arabella's wedding. I made my plans the next day.

We were sitting around the parlor after supper, Aunt Hattie and Folansbee working a jigsaw puzzle, Jack reading his newspaper.

"I'll bet you're sorry now," Janice said, "that you never listened to me. I'll bet you could kick yourself that Junior's got Arabella."

"Arabella's a lovely girl," Aunt Hattie said.

I ignored them. "I'm leaving Sunday," I said. "It will take me almost three days to drive back. I can take off right after the wedding."

"I have a wonderful idea," Janice said. "Why don't you kidnap Arabella at the wedding and take her with you? I'll bet she'd go."

Jack pulled his newspaper down and exposed his darkened face. "What are you talking about? Are you insane?"

"No! People do those things all the time. I think it would be very romantic and thrilling. Why don't you?"

"You never give up, do you?" I said, trying to smile. I was thinking that one day soon I would invite all in this room to Chicago to witness my own marriage to Nance.

The wedding took place in the small orchard at the back of the Badmington garden. I had my bag packed and in the car so I could take off right after the ceremony, and I arrived late. The church harpist was playing and everybody was lined up, making an aisle from the house out to the orchard. I walked slowly behind the guests and found a spot alone, at the end of the orchard under an apple tree, where I wouldn't have to talk to anybody. I winked encouragingly at Junior, who was already there, shifting from foot to foot and working his neck out of his collar. He was nervous. Hank, Sr., was standing next to him, having collar trouble, and his wife had already begun to cry. Somebody, I thought, has got to speak to this woman about the amount of starch she puts in shirts.

Arabella came out of the house with Mr. Badmington. They looked very solemn. As they walked slowly up the aisle, all the garden hats tipped and voices whispered that Arabella was a beautiful bride. She was. She looked unearthly beautiful and radiant.

The harpist came to the end of the piece, and Arabella stood next to Junior and faced the minister. There was an awful silence of transition while the minister looked over the crowd and cleared his throat and people coughed.

Arabella adjusted her gown, and Hank, Sr., picked up one of the flowers she dropped and handed it to her, and she whispered, "Thank you," to him. The minister raised his head, moistened his lips, and said, "We are gathered together this day. . . ."

Arabella had turned pale. There was an expression of near panic in her eyes, as if at any moment she might cry. Slowly, she turned her head and saw me, leaning against the tree, staring at her. I winked reassuringly, and she smiled, a trembling, weak smile.

Junior was in terrible shape. He wanted desperately to get out of that collar. His neck had become scarlet from the strain, and you could see the muscles tightening as if they were going to choke him. Hank, Sr., was evidently in serious trouble. He had put his finger inside his collar and was twisting his head in a circular motion, trying to free himself.

Watching the two of them, I automatically reached up and held my collar straight and bent my head in an effort to relax my neck muscles. When I looked up, I saw Arabella frowning at me. I stared at her for a long minute and then, by way of explanation, nodded in the direction of the two Hanks. Unobtrusively, Arabella turned and looked at them, at one and then the other, pushing their chins in and out in small, quick ties.

I knew immediately that what I had begun was terrible, but now, something wild and instinctive drove me on. I leaned back against the tree and stared directly at Arabella and half-closed my eyes and gave her that old look. Terrified, I knew there was no turning back.

For minutes, Arabella looked straight through me, as if she were suffering a pain so excruciating that she was unable to communicate it. Then, slowly, she forced her eyes away and looked at the minister. I could tell by her heavy breathing and the desperate, vacant look in her eyes that it was beginning to happen. As if an invisible hand had struck her, she closed her eyes and sucked in her cheeks and bit them. For a moment, she rocked back and forth, and then her eyes flew open and she stared at me in horror. Her shoulders drew up convulsively, the whiteness left her face in a quick flush, she dropped the flowers and threw her hands to her mouth and screamed. Then, as she looked back and forth from Junior to Hank, Sr., she fell helplessly into a fit of laughter.

It was beautiful laughter. It broke the tension in the orchard, and it set off my heart like a firecracker. The minister and the two Hanks were staring at her stupidly and that broke her up all the more. The garden hats were rocking and everybody was whispering, and it was perfectly apparent that Arabella's "trouble" had returned to betray her on her wedding day.

I could see chaos moving in, and I knew it was up to me to rescue Arabella. I took my bearings and plotted a course. I came at a fast clip, grabbed Arabella by the hand and pulled her after me. We were running through the orchard, past the stunned guests, Arabella laughing all the way, so weak that she could hardly make it. I paused at the house to let her get her breath, and we looked back and saw Junior coming after us.

"Please! Please, Hank," Arabella cried out. "Don't. I'm terribly sorry! It's . . . better this way. Really. I know it is."

That stopped him cold.

Arabella turned to me, the tears streaming down her face. "You've got to take me with you," she cried. "I can't stay in this town." She began to laugh again until she was so weak she couldn't even stand up. "You've ruined me forever!" I lifted her into my arms and carried her out and put her in the convertible and went around to the driver's seat. The front yard was filling with people, staring at us. "I'm terribly sorry!" Arabella called back. And then she looked at them and fell into another fit of laughter.

I gunned the motor and released the brake.

"Wait a minute! Wait a minute!" It was my sister Janice running down the steps of the Badmington house with Arabella's suitcase. She threw it in the backseat and hugged Arabella and kissed her. "Good-bye," she sobbed.

We took off, waving back at the crowd in the front yard. A few of them, hypnotized, raised their arms and waved stiffly. We drove out of the city and stopped late that night at a Justice of the Peace and were married. The next morning, we drove on toward Chicago.

Of course, it would be a shock to Nance, but I knew it wouldn't be five minutes before she'd have worked out an adjustment. "You simply pretend, dear, that life is a big, wonderful gamble, and if you lose, why perhaps it's better all around. There are simply lines of men dying to take you up the first moment they can, and it's like a game, angel, deciding who it will be and just how to go about it."

LATCH THE
DOOR LIGHTLY

Catharine Boyd

Marriage—vows said in a stain-glassed church, the Prince and Princess the center of attention, all the family and most close friends there—how easy then to sing those five words: "Till death do us part."

But the vision fades—and harsh realities replace them. Daily tugs-of-war: who gives in to whom today?

Well, Carol had had enough and asked for a divorce. . . . But somehow the "freedom" failed to bring her the happiness she assumed was a given. So it was, in long sleepless nights, that she began to think about those tugs-of-war—and who almost invariably won them.

*B*y noon on a January day the apartment at last stood empty, and Carol waited alone in the echoing rooms. She was a tall, dark, restless girl, brisk and determined; even the short curls that turned up over the edge of her small red hat were crisp and lively. She already wore her coat and gloves, and beside her were three suitcases of clothes for herself and the baby, a bundle of teddy bears and knitted blankets, and a portable phonograph. She stamped her foot impatiently for the porter. Out of here, quick!

The furniture, pictures—everything that had filled the three small rooms—was on its way to some anonymous vault for storage. There was nothing in the lot that either she or Tony had wished to salvage.

"I don't care what you do with any of it," Tony had said. "All I want is my electric razor."

And to tell the truth, his razor was just about all he had taken. A bag of clothing—but clothes meant nothing to him and he hadn't many. His camera, his precious tool chest, a box of souvenirs from his Army days. He had packed his things and vanished by cab that same evening over a month ago, and if he had later wished for some forgotten treasure, he never let Carol know.

She had talked to him only once since then, by telephone. He was off for California to set up a factory branch, and he asked her to wait to arrange settlement until he returned. She replied that the time was of no importance; she certainly had no plans for remarriage.

The elderly porter knocked, and Carol followed him down the hall to the elevator. Her steps were as light as a dancer's and her pulse raced; her elation was such that she might have been boarding a plane for Paris or sailing on a Caribbean cruise, though of course she was not. This was a journey of a different kind, a running back to her self. It was enough to know that her car was packed out front at the curb, for it held in its power the open sesame of escape.

She stopped at her first-floor neighbor's to pick up the baby. After the porter arranged her luggage in the trunk, he tipped his hat good-bye, nodding gravely. Then he gave her an odd, bewildered glance, for he saw that her face was serene.

Carol caught the look and pondered over it as she started to drive. The old man was right, of course; she was not behaving according to the rules. Women indulge in great emotional fuss at such moments, reluctant to lose what they have already cast away. Surely she should have betrayed some pang, some rush of tears, some sharp, nostalgic longing! Instead she felt only immense relief and satisfaction. She and Tony were through.

It was more than five hundred miles to Marystown, where her mother waited—and Grandma, and Amie, her closest friend—a trip requiring a night at a wayside motel, which turned it into kind of a gay adventure. The baby slept.

It's hard to believe, she thought as she drove. *How easy the parting!* The gradual stretching apart between them . . . like pulling taffy in opposite directions till only a wisp remains and curls away in the air. They simply had never agreed.

Tony used to say: "I can't give in on everything, darling, not *everything.* And one thing sure, I can't live penned up in this city flat forever!"

And Carol would answer: "Why do you have to call it a *flat?* Don't ask me to spend the rest of my days with the dandelions and rabbits. Just don't ask me again!"

But Tony persistently studied the real estate ads in the *Weekly Suburban,* smiling to himself. And just the sight of him wetting the tip of a pencil and drawing deliberate circles around certain "small country homes, magnificent view" was enough to make Carol's blood pound fiercely through her veins. She knew exactly the section of town where they ought to live—a charming cobblestone street in the heart of the busy central area, with all the advantages of the city as well as privacy.

There's simply no reason why he can't see my point of view, Carol brooded. *He's always been reasonable before when I was right. Now he won't even listen!*

So one night while they were going over the monthly budget—a perilous task, at best—they once again spoke of where they should buy their house, a matter to be taken seriously now that the bank account stood ready.

"It's time Sandy had a room of his own to grow up in," Tony began, "and a place to play. One bedroom isn't enough for a family. We'll end up with two or three cradles lined along the wall!"

"Not unless you stop talking nonsense," Carol answered firmly. "I will not move to the backwoods!"

Tony's jaw tightened, and he closed the account book with a sharp clap. "Nobody asked you to move to the backwoods, Carol," he said in a low, determined voice. "All I ask is a patch of grass and a tree and a place for Sandy to run. And I intend to have it."

Carol swayed at his tone, astonished to face all at once the possibility of defeat. In all the years of dispute and dissension it had never come to this.

"All right, Tony, let's be honest," she said calmly, trying to match his control. "We just can't get together on anything, even our home. We might as well end it now, for good. We're through."

It had been as easy as that, so easy that even she had been surprised. Except that Tony didn't believe her at first; and of course there was the problem of the baby.

"Well, what about my son?" Tony's first words had been, his face turning white as he understood she meant it. "What about Sandy?"

"He's young; it's better now than later," Carol had answered, holding her ground. "We'll never agree."

"Only when I agree with you," Tony said slowly, softly. "Carol, won't you take time? We can find a country place you'll like, I swear it!"

"No, no use," she declared. "Why torment ourselves longer? It's better over."

She half expected then some promise of yielding, some hint that a city house with a small back yard might do. If he cared so much, it seemed very little to ask! But Tony's mouth was rigid, his eyes steady and resolute.

"You know I'll insist on seeing Sandy," he stated clearly. "I'll have my rights written in."

"I want you to," Carol replied.

And now as she drove, she thought for a moment of the child, and she reached to touch his face. Dear heart, dear love, young Anthony Reeves—the physical evidence of a marriage set aside, the irrefutable proof that two lives had met for a while with common hopes and desires.

All at once she was overcome with weariness, and Sandy stretched and yawned beside her, mouthing for food. It was time to stop for the night. There would be no argument this time about the size or appearance or price of the motel. She could choose it herself.

Carol and Sandy reached Marystown the next afternoon at dusk; the street lamps on Elm went on as they turned the corner. Carol could see the two-story white frame house, the wide front porch obscured by a tangle of brown winter vines. How often she'd sat in a glider behind those vines on summer afternoons, playing dolls with Amie! And when she was older, she had sat on summer evenings with Tony, with Glenn . . . and finally with Tony. How sweet the shade, how placid the years ahead!

She bundled the baby out of his basket, went up the front steps, and quickly rang the bell. Her mother opened the door and held out her arms.

A wood fire burned in the living room, and Grandmother sat in a corner chair, her receding world around her. Her feet in their childish strap slippers rested on a stool, and her battered cane hung over the arm of her chair. She had grown very old and tiny, like a wizened doll.

"Never saw you look better," Grandmother said in a small and whispery voice. "Let me see the baby." She shifted her eyeglasses and examined him shrewdly. "The picture of Tony."

"Now, Mama, we agreed—" Carol's mother warned softly.

"Didn't agree to anything," Grandmother snapped. "No use acting as if the boy's father's dead, just because Carol left him. Always was willful!"

"Grandma, we just couldn't get along!" Carol said. "Please try to understand."

"Whole thing's a pack of nonsense," the old woman mumbled. "You never gave it a chance. Bert and me were married fifty-one years, and good reason for it. You think we frolicked along in tune all the way? No more'n anybody else. But one thing sure—I never closed the door without I left room to get back in!"

That night when Carol went upstairs, she settled deliciously under the familiar old quilt in the canopy bed and tried to become, for a moment or two, a girl again. The sounds and shadows that flavored the nights of her childhood returned. But the baby stirred in his crib beside her, and she could not remember just how she used to lie, for her body now curved in the shape she had learned during five years with Tony.

No, things are not the same, she thought drowsily. But Amie will be the same. Amie, who slept in this bed with me a hundred times, who shared my diaries and my room at college and was my only bridesmaid! Dear Amie . . .

Next morning she raced through her chores in high anticipation, and sat down at last to call her friend. The telephone rang twice before a faint voice answered.

"Hello? Amie, it's me!"

"Carol!" Amie's high, sweet voice cried back. "You're really home. I'm so sorry about you and Tony."

"How are things, Amie? How are Jack and the baby?"

"Wonderful, happy as lambs. When can we get together?"

"We might have lunch downtown today."

"Oh, today? Darling, I can't. Jack's bringing company home to dinner."

"Well, this weekend, then—Saturday, maybe?"

"This weekend? Well, I don't know . . . but we'll have to soon."

Amie's delicate voice was much the same, as silken and soft as the pale blonde hair that gave her that coveted angel look. But a note of reserve had crept beneath the surface warmth in her voice, and the best she could promise was lunch at her house the following week—please come . . . any day.

Carol sat by the phone awhile after she had hung up. Then she remembered that she must talk with her lawyer, and briskly dialed the number of Fogwell & Hurst.

On Thursday she dressed for her business appointment with particular care, as one always does for a former suitor. Glenn Fogwell was the tax partner in the firm that must handle her divorce, so she wore a little mascara, her prettiest earrings, an extra touch of perfume.

Glenn was waiting for her and drew her first into his own office, where they measured each other with desultory talk, avoiding the subject at hand. Glenn was a slender, dark young man, fastidiously groomed, tense and vitally ambitious—quite different from Tony. Carol had constantly compared the two men during her courting days. For several years, in fact, she had not favored one or the other, not till the very end—when all at once some endearing motion, some word, some special kiss had set Tony apart and she had fallen in love.

Glenn's telephone interrupted their visit, and he showed her next door, introduced her quickly to his partner and left them alone. She had not met Kenneth Hurst before, and she faced him across the desk with calculated coolness, girded against any well-meaning efforts at reconciliation. She stated the grounds for divorce, determined the state regulations and length of time required, asked about court procedure and fees involved, and promised to turn over Tony's stipulations regarding the child as soon as she received them.

As she passed down the hall later Glenn stepped out of his cubicle to say good-by. "Have lunch with me someday," he suggested without commitment—a young man wounded and healed, now safely armored. "We'll round up some of the crowd."

"Yes, call me," Carol answered, and quickened her pace. She stopped in the hallway to take off her sparkly earrings. If she had it to do all over again, she thought, she would still choose Tony.

Carol applied for a job at the telephone office, where she had worked before her marriage; and after a week on Elm Street she decided to find a place of her own downtown, in the heart of things. The old house contained enough beds and chairs and bureaus, perhaps, and rooms for them all. But it takes a very large house indeed to span four generations.

She was chagrined to find that her mother did not urge her to stay, and Carol felt cast adrift.

"I couldn't allow you to stay too long," her mother said, smiling. "I have to remind myself constantly that the generations have shifted. You are no longer the child; you are now the mother. If we were together, things might become confused. You know that's true." She touched her daughter's arm gently.

The chosen apartment was reasonably clean—except for the dreary, cavernous court it faced upon—and unreasonably compact. It was also starkly furnished: bare walls, undraped windows, empty tables, not even a bookcase. It occurred to Carol that if Tony were here, he could very likely build a bookcase for the empty corner. He liked to work with his hands, and he was forever buying new tools and sending off for furniture plans. But somehow he seldom got further than dreaming about these things. He knew how she hated the noise and the clutter, for she was tidy by nature; he finally let her buy a ready-made toy chest for Sandy. And she now remembered uneasily how often he had got out his new power saw, cleaned it and oiled it and lovingly tested the blade, and put it away. She set this thought aside.

Once established, Carol tallied her resources. She had known that divorce was expensive, but it was appalling how many small debts she had already acquired for which she was now solely accountable.

I'll have to buy curtains and one or two prints for the wall, she said to herself. I'll have a yellow living room again, like we had before. I wonder why Tony always wanted blue? . . . She leafed through her checkbook, hoping she had made a mistake, but she had not. Her first month's rent was paid and her balance was frighteningly low. Baby care would cost a lot, and tailored clothes for the office. The dentist's appointment could wait another month.

She hustled around the new rooms; her mind worked faster while her hands were busy. Why, I'll sell my car, of course! she decided on impulse. There's a bus at the corner I can take to work. She promptly reached for the classified telephone book.

The car was worth very little; why, it was scarcely worth selling! The dealers all said, "A year or two ago . . ." and she thus unwillingly recalled that Tony had wanted to make the trade-in two years ago when values were high and that she had rebelled.

"It's our honeymoon car. I won't give it up!" she had cried. "I want to keep it! Please, darling, please?" So Tony had acquiesced, with some good-natured joke about its heirloom value forty years hence. "Who knows, it may be worth a fortune!" he'd said, grinning. "Hang on to it, sweetie, if it keeps you happy."

She now accepted the modest sum she was offered; there was no choice.

A personnel job at the telephone office was open for Carol, starting the following week. Since she had only one free day before reporting for work, she dressed the baby and took the bus to Amie's for lunch.

Amie and Jack owned a small-development house in Brynhurst, a brick-faced house like a hundred others, with picture window, lamppost, and picket fence all around to keep the babies in.

"We don't like it much, but in two or three years we'll do better," Amie explained at the door. "There's a brown-shingled house for sale at the end of the road, with a rose garden already planted and half an acre of woods."

"How gruesome," Carol said. She had passed this house on her way from the bus, one of those rustic little gems that Tony was always reading about.

"Well, come in, come in!"

Amie was small and gentle, about up to Carol's chin; she liked lots of ruffles and ribbons but had trouble keeping them pressed. Her two-year-old son was beating muffin tins in the playpen. Carol set Sandy down beside him and stood back to admire them both.

"Amie, he's beautiful!" she declared. "Jack must adore him."

"Yes," Amie answered in an odd voice. "Yes, he does." And she burst into tears.

"What in the world?" Carol asked in astonishment, taking off her coat. "We'd better sit down."

"It's nothing—only seeing you again," Amie sobbed. "You always took charge of things, told me what to do—you know how it was."

"Sounds pretty bossy of me," Carol answered wryly.

"It's just that Jack and I had a terrible fuss this morning," Amie continued. "Jack gets so mad about little things like dust and wrinkles. And I get so furious being cooped up I can hardly stand it. I'm so tired of everything. If I could only walk out—like you!"

"Now, that's ridiculous," Carol replied calmly. "You're just upset. You don't really want to walk out, or you would."

"But I can't!" Amie answered, wide-eyed, gathering her defenses. "Every time I get ready to leave, something silly happens. I realize my only good dress is at the cleaners, or the baby has been exposed to measles, or I just plain don't have any *money*. So I sit around and think about it for a while." She wiped her eyes. "And when Jack comes home at night he's sorry and sweet, and—you know how it is. Things blow over."

"It's strange, but I thought you and Jack were perfect together," Carol said. "How do you stand it?"

"I've already told you." Amie began to smile, thinking about the rosy reunion in store for that evening. "I guess lots of women wish they could walk out once in a while. Only we don't have any money and any place to go, and babies . . . and maybe it's just as well. Because after we stop being mad, everything's all right. Jack's always so wonderful!"

Carol threw up her hands. "Oh, you're hopeless," she said, laughing. "You never could make up your mind! But if you ever need someplace to go, sweetie, move in with me!"

On Wednesday Carol started back to work with great excitement. A middle-aged woman, retired from nursing, took Sandy into her home by the day; he would have to be delivered at quarter of nine and picked up at quarter after five, and Carol would have to accomplish this by bus, since she no longer had a car.

She soon discovered that working was more of a chore than it had been when she was single. There was neither a mother nor a

grandmother to air the rooms and whisk through the laundry. . . .
But neither was there anyone to complain if she felt tired or lazy
and let things go.

I must start having friends in, she decided firmly. For my
self-respect. I'll start with Amie and Jack.

And so she did. A young widow in her office made a willing
fourth for bridge, and once in a while she coaxed two more
couples in for a second table. Her parties were gay; she served
good food, played cheerful music, and brightened the background with flowers and lighted candles.

"It's always so perfect here," Amie would tell her with envy.
"So peaceful—no tension or quarrels." Jack and Amie often
stayed for a nightcap after the others had gone, and when it was
time to leave they did so with their arms around each other, and
afterward the apartment seemed quite desolate indeed.

Party post-mortems with Tony were always fun, Carol would
think as she straightened up the quiet room. He never cared for
parties much, but he took them in stride. Remember the time
he gave up his annual fishing club weekend because of a special
party? This thought was somehow uncomfortable, looking back
upon it, for she realized, against her will, that this same dispute
had been settled two years in a row by Tony's good-humored
compliance. She had almost forgotten.

It's true that the best part of pleasure is sharing it, she admitted,
but only to herself.

She would not admit to Amie or her mother or anyone else
the echoes that haunted the lonely hours while Sandy slept. Nor
would she care to confess that there were nights when she crept
home from work so exhausted that the evening chores, even an
hour's play with the baby, were almost beyond her strength, and
all she could manage for dinner was a peanut-butter sandwich.

She also stopped drinking coffee at night and began to have hot lemonade or a cup of cocoa instead. Nevertheless, when she climbed into bed, she lay fitfully awake, hour after hour. She would pile on a blanket and still another, sternly denying the fact that she ached for the warmth of Tony's arms.

Physical, that's all, she'd whisper to herself. I knew I'd miss this part—though I didn't know how much. It isn't fair to eat the icing and throw the cake away, as some women do. . . . But once in a while, for all her reasoning, the longing assailed her in waves of pain.

"I *cannot* understand people putting up with conflict day after day just because they like to make love!" she once told Amie sharply. "That's not enough for marriage!"

"Well, sometimes it helps," Amie said with a sigh.

Carol began to enjoy the weekend trips to Brynhurst to visit Amie. Riding the bus, she would watch for the first row of trees, the first wide field of grass. She would point out the skittering squirrels to Sandy, the kites and fire engines. The road to Amie's led past the empty brown-shingled house, and each time she passed it Carol smiled with relief because Tony was not there to be lured by the real-estate signs and the shutters that needed paint.

The shingled house became a symbol of all the rural nonsense she had so narrowly escaped. Once she took Sandy inside the gate and let him pick some of the clover that sweetened the long grass. And once she saw the front door ajar and wandered inside, aghast at the ancient plumbing and heaving floors. She supposed a great deal could be done to the place by a man like Tony. But why, when a modern town house would save the muss and trouble?

When she reached Amie's, they would walk with the children,

or rest in the spring sunshine that warmed the small back yard. Carol tried to avoid Jack and Amie when they were together, for the visible warmth between them left her disturbed and discontented. How could Amie, so often dissolved in tearful rages, so swiftly surrender to temporary truce? On the other hand, if such a state of compromise was possible, perhaps things balanced out over the years—the happy times, the moments of indescribable rapport. Perhaps even she and Tony, if he had not been so obstinate . . .

The first week in May had nothing to do with warbling birds and trees like pink clouds against a clean spring sky. In the close-curtained, tidy rooms where Carol lived, a series of small catastrophes piled one upon the other all the way from Monday.

First there were such things as the kitchen sink backing up, an overdue bill and a reprimand at the office. Then on Wednesday Sandy became ill with a frightening cold, and Carol spent two sleepless nights, half ill herself, fighting the fever and her solitary panic. Tony would have promptly called the doctor, but she could not, for the doctor would say, *Where's your husband? Call your mother. Get someone in to help.* And there was no one.

Because she was weak and lightheaded with fatigue, not quite herself, she kept reliving the last time she'd had a fever, the ice packs and fresh pillowcases, and the anxious, comforting hands of her husband. It seemed to be more than illness harassing her now; something was crumpling inside her, something that once held her courage and principles together, demanding perfection. She was no longer so sure about divorce, even when two people didn't always get along. She wanted Tony.

On Friday morning the baby wakened well and beaming, and while he was having breakfast, Tony called. He was back East on business and wanted to see his son. It had been five months, and Sandy already had shoes with soles to toddle in; of course Tony wanted to see him.

By six o'clock that evening the living room glowed its welcome; the baby was bathed and dressed, rocking contentedly in his canvas play chair. Then Carol hurried to prepare herself, flying from bureau to bathroom mirror—petticoat, necklace, silk sheath dress, brushed-up shining curls, a mist of perfume. She was slipping into her sandals when she heard the bell, and she thought: Oh, no, not Tony so soon!

But Tony was there, hat tipped back, arms full of presents for Sandy. He dropped his coat and his gifts on the sofa and held out his arms to his son.

"Real shoes. What do you know!" Tony said, laughing. "Getting plenty of groceries, fellow?"

"He's had a touch of flu, but he's better now," Carol explained.

Tony scooped up the child, who crowed and tossed his head in delight and finally settled astride his father's knee.

"He could use some country air. But you look well established," Tony observed. "I see you've got another yellow room—" he laughed agreeably—"like ours."

"I'm sorry," Carol answered quickly. Now, what kind of answer was that? She wasn't sorry! The yellow room had been her first triumph in their marriage, a great satisfaction. They had parried the issue back and forth for more than a week, till Tony said at last: "All right, baby, go ahead with yellow if it means so much. Though I still like blue." She had won her own way, hadn't she? Wasn't that what she wanted?

"Oh, by the way, these papers—" Tony laid an envelope on

the sofa. "They go to Mr. Hurst. I understand the decree is due in another month."

"Yes," Carol answered faintly.

He held the child awhile, talking distantly about the California job. He asked about Mother and Grandma and Amie and Jack and even Glenn, and finally went off to put his son to bed.

When he came back Carol's lipstick was brighter, and two cups had been arranged side by side on the coffee table. He reached for his coat and scarf. "Tea?" he asked, surprised. "I thought you never drank it."

"No, but you do," Carol answered, and at the same time, she absently reached to adjust his scarf, and her hand brushed his cheek. He hesitated, drawing in his breath; his glance met hers swiftly and recoiled. Then he crossed his scarf over his chest and buttoned his coat.

"Sorry," he said. "My plane takes off at nine."

Oh, stay a moment! she begged with her eyes. *Stay awhile, talk to me, scold me, argue with me, only stay!*

He gave her a guarded, stranger's smile and turned away.

After he was gone Carol rested her flushed cheek against the cool white paint of the door, the papers clutched in her hand. She stood for a long time, turning them over and over. It is easy to say, I will leave. And sometimes the parting is easy; even the living alone is a brave adventure. But sometime, somewhere along the way, a moment strikes the heart with terror, with wild dismay: It's really over! No—I didn't mean it! Let me back in!

Tomorrow she'd take Tony's papers down to her lawyer. No, she would wait till Monday. Perhaps if she lingered—what if she lost them?—things might be postponed. Perhaps she might fend off the final decree, at least for a while.

Tony would come back for Sandy. He might even follow the

path of remembered longing into her arms. But why would he stay? Be honest, Carol. Think back. To set aside his gleaming power saw unused? To give up his fishing club for her dinner parties? To sit in a yellow living room because it pleased her? To yield on every issue all the rest of their lives? He had, so far—except for the house.

So why would he stay, to languish behind curtained courtyard windows in a city apartment?

The weight of the truth, borne all at once, was a staggering burden, and Carol's mind drifted off to escape it. But she kept seeing the gardens and gateways along the road to Amie's and thinking: "A pleasant way to live. Pleasant for children to scamper in the sunshine, pleasant for husbands who like to climb ladders and rake leaves and put new paint on shutters. And suddenly she *knew:* the brown-shingled house! The brown-shingled house!

I want that house! she thought fiercely; she still made quick decisions. *I want it for him. I've got to be living in that house the next time Tony visits! How soon can I make it? How much will I have to pay down?*

Her thoughts pinwheeled with excitement, soared with hope. The grass needs cutting out there; I wanted to cut that grass the first time I saw it. And Tony could have his own workshop, workbench and all, in the shed out back. He could make that place like new in a couple of years. I'd even help him . . . if I had a chance.

She was overwhelmed by a feeling of warmth and happiness that amazed her; in all the times that Tony had let her have her way she never remembered this sense of exultation.

The baby was crying. She went to the crib and lifted him over her shoulder with a special hug, and holding him close, she answered the ring of the telephone.

"Carol, it's me—it's Amie," a voice cried. "I'm leaving Jack! I'm already packed. This time I mean it. I'm closing the door."

"Be quiet. You're acting like a child," Carol answered sternly. "Start unpacking—before Jack calls your bluff."

There was a startled pause.

"What do you mean?" Amie asked in consternation. "You told me once I could come to your place—you know you did!"

"I've learned a lot since then," Carol said. "Now listen to me. You're not coming here, for I won't let you in. Understand?"

"But, Carol, I have no place else where I can go."

"Then sit down and take some time to think things over. At least till tomorrow. You hear me, Amie?"

"Carol, you know what'll happen, just like always," Amie cried, but her voice was already calmer. "You know I can't resist Jack, and he's always so sorry and sweet afterward, and by tomorrow morning I won't even want to go!"

"Yes, that's exactly what I mean," Carol said. "This time and the next."

Then she hung up the telephone and sat for a while in her yellow room, rocking the baby, alone.

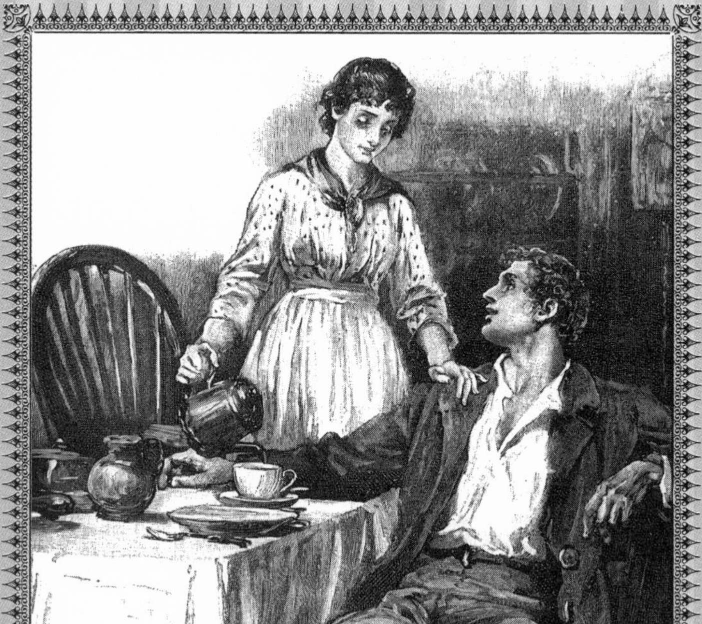

JOHNNY LINGO'S
EIGHT-COW WIFE

Patricia McGerr

How the villagers laughed. The sharpest trader in the islands finally got taken by a woman yet! But Johnny didn't answer them. Let them laugh all they wanted. He had his reasons. A visitor to the island just had to look at this poor bargain for herself.

*M*any things can change a woman. Things that happen inside; things that happen outside. But few things matter more than what she thinks about herself.

When I sailed to Kiniwata, an island in the Pacific, I took along a notebook. After I got back, it was filled with descriptions of flora and fauna, native customs and costumes. But the only note that still interests me is the one that says: "Johnny Lingo gave eight cows to Sarita's father." And I don't need to have it in writing. I'm reminded of it every time I see a woman belittling her husband or a wife withering under her husband's scorn. I want to say to them, "You should know why Johnny Lingo paid eight cows for his wife."

Johnny Lingo wasn't exactly his name. But that's what Shenkin, the manager of the guest house on Kiniwata, called him. Shenkin was from Chicago and had a habit of Americanizing the names of the islanders. But Johnny was mentioned by many people in many connections. If I wanted to spend a few days on the neighboring island of Murabandi, Johnny Lingo could put me up. If I wanted to fish, he could show me where the biting was best. If it was pearls I sought, he would bring me the best buys. The people of Kiniwata all spoke highly of Johnny Lingo. Yet when they spoke they smiled, and the smiles were slightly mocking.

"Get Johnny Lingo to help you find what you want and let him do the bargaining," advised Shenkin. "Johnny knows how to make a deal."

"Johnny Lingo!" The boy seated nearby hooted the name and rocked with laughter.

"What goes on?" I demanded. "Everybody tells me to get in touch with Johnny Lingo and then breaks up. Let me in on the joke."

"Oh, the people like to laugh," Shenkin said, shrugging. "Johnny's the brightest, the strongest young man in the islands. And for his age, the richest."

"But if he's all you say, what is there to laugh about?"

"Only one thing. Five months ago, at fall festival, Johnny came to Kiniwata and found himself a wife. He paid her father eight cows!"

I knew enough about island customs to be impressed. Two or three cows would buy a fair-to-middling wife, four or five a highly satisfactory one.

"Good Lord!" I said. "Eight cows! She must have beauty that takes your breath away."

"She's not ugly," he conceded, and smiled a little. "But the kindest could only call Sarita plain. Sam Karoo, her father, was afraid she'd be left on his hands."

"But then he got eight cows for her? Isn't that extraordinary?"

"Never been paid before."

"Yet you call Johnny's wife plain?"

"I said it would be kindness to call her plain. She was skinny. She walked with her shoulders hunched and her head ducked. She was scared of her own shadow."

"Well," I said, "I guess there's just no accounting for love."

"True enough," agreed the man. "And that's why the villagers grin when they talk about Johnny. They get special satisfaction from the fact that the sharpest trader in the islands was bested by dull old Sam Karoo."

"But how?"

"No one knows and everyone wonders. All the cousins were urging Sam to ask for three cows and hold out for two until he was sure Johnny'd pay only one. Then Johnny came to Sam

Karoo and said, 'Father of Sarita, I offer eight cows for your daughter.'"

"Eight cows," I murmured. "I'd like to meet this Johnny Lingo."

I wanted fish. I wanted pearls. So the next afternoon I beached my boat at Nurabandi. And I noticed as I asked directions to Johnny's house that his name brought no sly smile to the lips of his fellow Nurabandians. And when I met the slim, serious young man, when he welcomed me with grace to his home, I was glad that from his own people he had respect unmingled with mockery. We sat in his house and talked. Then he asked. "You come here from Kiniwata?"

"Yes."

"They speak of me on that island?"

"They say there's nothing I might want that you can't help me get."

He smiled gently. "My wife is from Kiniwata."

"Yes, I know."

"They speak of her?"

"A little."

"What do they say?"

"Why, just . . ." The question caught me off balance. "They told me you were married at festival time."

"Nothing more?" The curve of his eyebrows told me he knew there had to be more.

"They also say the marriage settlement was eight cows." I paused. "They wonder why."

"They ask that?" His eyes lighted with pleasure. "Everyone in Kiniwata knows about the eight cows?"

I nodded.

"And in Nurabandi everyone knows it too." His chest

expanded with satisfaction. "Always and forever, when they speak of marriage settlements, it will be remembered that Johnny Lingo paid eight cows for Sarita."

So that's the answer, I thought: *vanity.*

And then I saw her. I watched her enter the room to place flowers on the table. She stood still a moment to smile at the young man beside me. Then she went swiftly out again. She was the most beautiful woman I had ever seen. The lift of her shoulders, the tilt of her chin, the sparkle of her eyes all spelled a pride to which no one could deny her the right.

I turned back to Johnny Lingo and found him looking at me.

"You admire her?" he murmured.

"She . . . she's glorious. But she's not Sarita from Kiniwata," I said.

"There's only one Sarita. Perhaps she does not look the way they say she looked in Kiniwata."

"She doesn't. I heard she was homely. They all make fun of you because you let yourself be cheated by Sam Karoo."

"You think eight cows were too many?" A smile slid over his lips.

"No. But how can she be so different?"

"Do you ever think," he asked, "what it must mean to a woman to know that her husband has settled on the lowest price for which she can be bought? And then later, when the women talk, they boast of what their husbands paid for them. One says four cows, another maybe six. How does she feel, the woman who was sold for one or two? This could not happen to my Sarita."

"Then you did this just to make your wife happy?"

"I wanted Sarita to be happy, yes. But I wanted more than that. You say she is different. This is true. Many things can change a woman. Things that happen inside, things that happen outside. But the thing that matters most is what she thinks about herself. In Kiniwata, Sarita believed she was worth nothing. Now she knows she is worth more than any other woman in the islands."

"Then you wanted—"

"I wanted to marry Sarita. I loved her and no other woman.

"But," he finished softly, "I wanted an eight-cow wife."

THE SLIP-OVER
SWEATER

Jesse Stuart

*Shan is in love with the most popular girl in the high
school, Jo-Anne; in years gone by, his heart had belonged
to his neighbor, Grace. In this story, Shan makes a
choice—and reaps the results.*

*N*ow, if you don't get the sweater," Grace said as she followed me up the narrow mountain path, "you mustn't feel too badly. Everybody in Gadsen High School knows that you've made your letters. Just because you don't wear them like the other boys . . ."

Grace stopped talking before she finished the last sentence. And I knew why. But I didn't say anything—not right then. I stopped a minute to look down over the cliffs into the gorge where the mountain water swirled over the rocks, singing a melancholy song without words. Grace walked over and stood beside me. I knew the sound of the roaring water did the same thing to her that it did to me. We stood there watching this clear blue mountain water hit and swirl over the giant water-beaten rocks, splashing into spray as it had done for hundreds of years before we were born.

The large yellow-gold leaves sifted slowly down from the tall poplars. And the leaves fell like big soft red raindrops from low bushy-topped sourwoods to ferny ground. Dark frostbitten oak leaves slithered down among the lacework of tree branches to the leaf-carpeted ground. Two of these oak leaves dropped onto Grace's ripe-wheat-colored hair. And a big yellow-gold poplar leaf fell and stuck to my shirt. They were a little damp for they fell from a canopy of leaves where there was no sun.

Gold poplar leaves would look good in Jo-Anne Burton's chestnut-colored hair, I thought. *And how pretty the dark oak leaves would look on her blouse.* I was sorry she wasn't with me instead of Grace. I could just see Jo-Anne standing there with the red and yellow leaves falling on her.

I would say, "Gee, you look wonderful with those golden leaves in your hair."

"Do you think so?" she would answer. And I could imagine

her smile and her even white teeth. She was always gay and laughing.

I didn't say anything to Grace, but Grace knew how I felt about Jo-Anne. Grace and I had gone to Plum Grove grade school together for eight years. I had carried her books from the time I could remember. And then we started walking five miles across the mountains to Gadsen High School together. When we started to Gadsen I was still carrying her books. I'd carried them down and up this mountain for three years. But I was not carrying her books this year, and I wouldn't be again, for Gadsen was a bigger school than Plum Grove and there were many more girls. But there was only one for me, and Grace knew who she was. She was the prettiest and the most popular girl in Gadsen High School. When she was a sophomore, she was elected May Queen.

Grace knew why I wanted the slip-over sweater. It wasn't just to show the letters and the three stripes on the sleeve I'd won playing football three years for the Gadsen Tigers. Grace knew that Roy Tomlinson had a slip-over sweater and that he was trying to beat my time with Jo-Anne Burton. Grace had heard about Jo-Anne asking me one day why I didn't get a sweater.

"You've got a small waist and broad shoulders," Jo-Anne had said, "and you'd look wonderful in a slip-over sweater!"

I didn't care about having a sweater until Jo-Anne had said this to me. Now I wanted it more than anything on earth. I wanted a good one, of the style, color, and brand the other boys had bought. Then I could have my G and the three stripes sewed on, as my teammates had done. They let their favorite girls wear their sweaters. Jo-Anne was wearing Roy Tomlinson's, and that hurt me.

Grace probably knew I was thinking of Jo-Anne now. And as

she stood beside me, with the leaves falling onto her dress, I couldn't keep from thinking how they would look on Jo-Anne.

Why we had stopped at this high place every morning and evening for three years, I didn't know. But it was from here on the coldest days in winter, when the gorge below was a mass of ice, that we listened to the water singing its lonesome song beneath the ice. And here in early April we watched spring come back to the mountains.

We knew which trees leafed first. And even before the leaves came back we found trailing arbutus that had sprung up beside the cliffs and bloomed. Then came the percoon that sprang from the loamy coves where old logs had laid and rotted. It was the prettiest of all wildwood flowers and its season was short. Grace and I had taken bouquets of this to our high-school teachers before a sprig of green had come to the town below.

Grace shook the multicolored leaves from her hair and dress when we silently turned to move away. And I brushed the leaves from my shirtsleeves and trousers. We started up the mountain as we had done for the past three years—only I used to take Grace's arm. Now I walked in front and led the way. If there was a snake across the path, I took care of him. I just protected Grace as any boy would protect a girl he had once loved but had ceased to love since he had found another girl who meant more to him than anyone else in the world.

"If I had the money," Grace said after our long silence, "I'd let you have it, Shan, to buy your sweater."

"I'll get the money some way," I said.

Not another word was spoken while we climbed toward the ridge. But I did a lot of thinking. I was trying to figure out how I could buy that sweater. I was not going to hunt and trap wild animals any more and sell their skins just to get clothing for my own skin. Books had changed me since I'd gone to high school. I'd never have the teachers send me home because I had polecat scent on me. I'd always bought my schoolbooks and my clothes by hunting and trapping. But I'd not done it this year and I'd not do it again. I was determined about that. Books had made me want to do something in life—for my girl. And I knew now that I wanted to be a schoolteacher and teach math in Gadsen High School. And that's what I'd do.

When Grace started from the path across to her home, a big double-log house on Seaton Ridge, she said good-bye. And I said good-bye to her. These were the only words spoken. We used to linger a long time at this spot by a big oak tree. I looked over at the heart cut in the bark of the oak. Her initials and mine were cut side by side inside the heart. Now, if I'd had my knife, I would have gone over and shaved these initials and the heart from the oak bark. Now I hoped that she would find some boy she could love as much as I loved Jo-Anne.

When I first realized I had to get that sweater for Jo-Anne, I had thought about asking Pa for ten dollars. But I knew he wouldn't have it, for he raised light Burley tobacco, like Grace's father, and it hadn't been a good season. Pa had not made enough to buy winter clothes for my four brothers and six sisters. And another thing, I'd never in my life asked him for money. I'd made my own way. I'd told my father I'd do this if he'd only let me go to high school. He wasn't much on education. But he agreed to this, and I'd stick to my end of the bargain.

That night I thought about the people I knew. I wondered if I could borrow from one of them. I didn't like to borrow, but I'd do anything to get Jo-Anne to take off Roy Tomlinson's sweater and to put mine on in place of it. Most of the people I knew did not have the money, though.

At noon the next day the idea came to me: What are banks for? Their job is to lend money to needy people—and that's why I walked straight to the Citizens' State Bank at lunchtime. I was a citizen, a student at Gadsen High School, and I needed the money to buy a sweater. If Mr. Cole asked me why I needed the money, I'd just tell him I wanted very much to buy myself a sweater so I could put my school letter on it and my three stripes—and be like the other high-school boys. I wouldn't mention Jo-Anne.

I stood nervously at the window. Mr. Cole was a big heavy man with blue eyes and a pleasant smile. "Something I can do for you?" he asked politely.

"Yes, sir," I stammered, "I'd like to have ten dollars."

"You want to borrow it?" he asked.

"Yes, sir." Now the worst was over and my voice was calmer.

"You go to high school, don't you?"

"Yes, sir."

"Thought I'd seen you around here," he said. "You're the star player on the Gadsen Tigers—you're Mick Stringer's boy."

"Yes, sir," I said.

"What's your first name?" He started making out a note for me.

"Shan," I said. "Shan Stringer."

He shoved the note forward for me to sign. And he didn't ask for anyone to go my security. If he had, I don't know who I could have got to sign. I wasn't old enough to borrow money at the bank. But it just seemed to me as if Mr. Cole read my thought. He knew I wanted the money badly. So he gave me nine dollars and seventy-five cents and took a quarter for interest.

"This note will be due in three months," he said. "This is October twenty-eighth. Come back January twenty-eighth. And if you can't pay it then, I'll let you renew for another three months. And then we'll expect all or partial payment."

"Thank you, Mr. Cole."

I hurried to Womack Brothers store and bought the sweater. It had a red body with white sleeves—the Gadsen High colors. I would have Mom sew the white G on the front and the red stripes on the sleeves as soon as I got home. I was the happiest boy in the world. Gadsen High School had always been a fine place, but now it was wonderful. I loved everybody, but I worshiped Jo-Anne Burton.

That afternoon when Grace and I walked through the town and came to the mountain path, we talked more than we had in a long time. But I didn't mention what was in the package I was carrying. We stopped at our place on the cliffs and looked down at the swirling waters in the gorge. The dashing water did not sound melancholy to me. It was swift dance music like a reel from old Scotland. Even the trees above us with their arms interlaced were in love. All the world was in love because I had got what I wanted and I was in love.

The next morning Grace was waiting for me beside the old oak where we had cut our initials. Grace was all right, I thought. She was almost sure to be valedictorian of our class, and she was good-looking too. But she didn't have the kind of beauty Jo-Anne had. Jo-Anne was not only beautiful—she was always happy, laughing and showing her pretty teeth. She wasn't one of the best students in the class—her grades were not high at all. But she was friendly with everybody and as free as the wind. Her clothes were always pretty, and they fitted her much better than Grace's did. I loved the way she wore her clothes. I loved everything about Jo-Anne. She held my love as firmly as the mountain loam held the roots of the wild flowers and the big trees.

"Why are you taking that bundle back to school?" Grace asked.

"Oh, just to be carrying something," I said.

Grace laughed as though she thought I was very funny.

We got to school early. When I had a chance to speak to Jo-Anne alone, I told her what I had.

"Oh, Shan!" she exclaimed. "Oh, you're a darling!"

"Brand-new," I said. "You'll like it, Jo-Anne."

"Oh, I know I'll love it," she said. "I'll put it right on!"

I handed her the package and she hurried off. I was never happier in my life. When she came back, she was smiling at me, her eyes dancing. She walked over to Roy Tomlinson and handed a package to him. Everybody standing around was looking at Jo-Anne in the new sweater with the three stripes on the sleeve—the only sweater in the school with three stripes. Was Jo-Anne proud! And I was proud!

"Do you like it on me?" she asked as she walked up to me.

"Do I like it?" I said. "I love it."

She smiled happily, and I was glad that Roy could see now that I was the one Jo-Anne loved. And everybody knew now that I was in love with her. Roy would probably wonder, I was thinking, how I was able to buy that sweater. He had probably thought that he would be able to keep Jo-Anne with his sweater and his two stripes because I'd never be able to buy one for her. But Roy would never know how I got it—that would be a secret between Mr. Cole, the banker, and me.

While the girls were admiring the sweater and many of my teammates were looking on, I glanced over at Roy. He stood by, not saying a word, just looking at the sweater that had replaced his. I hadn't expected him to react that way, but in a few minutes Grace came in, and she was wearing Roy Tomlinson's sweater.

"Boy!" Jim Darby exclaimed. "Look at Grace! Doesn't that sweater look swell on her!"

"She isn't the same girl!" Ed Patton said.

I stared at Grace. I didn't realize a sweater could make such a difference. Her clothes had never become her. But this sweater did! There were many whispers and a lot of excitement as we flocked into the auditorium. I was watching Grace move through the crowd in her new sweater when Jo-Anne edged over close to me.

"You do like this sweater on me, don't you, Shan?" she asked.

"Sure do, Jo-Anne," I said. And I walked proudly beside her into the auditorium.

That afternoon after I had said good-bye to Jo-Anne, I looked around for Grace. She was just saying her good-bye to Roy. When she turned toward me, I could see that she was as proud of that sweater as she could be. And Roy stood there looking after us as we started toward the mountain together.

We stopped at the gorge, but we didn't stay long. Grace did most of the talking and I did the listening, but I didn't hear everything she said. I was wild with joy, for I was thinking about Jo-Anne wearing my new red sweater.

At every football game Jo-Anne sat on the front bleacher and yelled for me. And Grace yelled for Roy Tomlinson. Once when I made an eighty-five-yard run for a touchdown, Jo-Anne came up to me after the game and kissed me. I could outkick, outpass, and outrun Roy Tomlinson. And I didn't brag when I said it. He earned another stripe that season and so did I. Grace sewed Roy's third stripe on his sweater with pride. She kept the sweater clean as a pin. I'll have to admit she kept it cleaner than Jo-Anne kept mine.

When Grace was almost sure to be valedictorian, Roy Tomlinson could hardly stand the idea of our walking over the mountain together. He walked with us to the edge of Gadsen. But he never climbed the mountain and looked down at the gorge. He could just as well have come along. His going with her didn't bother me, not exactly. She did of course seem close to me—like a sister. As we walked along together I saw the trees along the ridge where we had had our playhouses and grapevines of trailing arbutus and percoon. And those initials on the oak reminded me of the days when we were little.

It was in the basketball season, just before the regional tournament, when I received a notice from the bank that my note was due. With the other little expenses I had at school, even twenty-five cents wasn't easy to get.

If the interest is hard to get, I thought, what will I do about the principal? What if I have to take the sweater from Jo-Anne and sell it to make a payment on the principal?

But when my mother let me have fifty cents and I paid the interest, I felt much better and didn't think about it again during the basketball season. Jo-Anne came to every game and was always urging everybody else to come. She was proud of me and the way I played as I was proud of her and the way she looked in my sweater.

Grace was never so talkative and gay and popular as Jo-Anne, and I was always glad to hear anyone pay Grace compliments. I heard Harley Potters say one day, "You know, Grace Hinton is a beautiful girl. Think, she comes five miles to school and five miles home and makes the highest grades in her class. There's something to a girl that would go through all kinds of weather and do that."

I thought so too. All through the winters when snow was on the ground and the winds blew harshly on the mountain, she and I had walked back and forth to school. I walked in front and broke the path through new fallen snow. I had done that even when we went to Plum Grove. We had walked through the rain and sleet together and I couldn't remember a day that she had not been good-natured. And I knew she had the durability and toughness of a storm-battered mountain oak. I didn't believe there was another girl in Gadsen High School who could have done what Grace had done. And now to the Gadsen boys and girls she was as pretty as a cove sapling. Yet I was sure I would never go back to Grace. I'd always love Jo-Anne.

I only hoped that Roy Tomlinson appreciated Grace. I got a little tired of looking at his sweater so often. Sometimes I wondered if I were jealous of him for making his third stripe. But I was sure I wasn't because I had four, and I had the most popular and beautiful girl in the world. I decided I was tired of looking at it just because Grace never wore anything else. I could hardly remember what Grace's clothes had looked like before.

When the heavy snows of January and February passed away in melted snow and rain down the gorge in deep foaming waters, I grew as melancholy as the song of this swollen little winter river. Jo-Anne didn't know what was worrying me. Sometimes I wished she would ask but she never did. And that hurt me too. If I didn't always smile at something she said, she acted impatient with me. I'm sure I could not have told her about the note due in April, if she had asked. But I looked for some kind of sympathy because I thought I needed it and that she loved me so much she would want to cheer me up. Instead, she kept asking me if I didn't love her, and if I did, why didn't I show it the way all the other boys did?

So I tried my best to cheer up. I didn't want to lose her, but I did have to figure out some way to make money. I couldn't hunt now even if I'd change my mind about killing animals. Spring was on the way, and animal pelts weren't good now.

One day Grace said to me, "What is the matter with you, Shan?" That was in late March, and we were watching the blue melted snow waters roll down the gorge where the white dog-wood sprays bent down to touch them. "I know something is bothering you."

"No, it isn't," I said. "I'm all right."

"If I can ever help you, I'll be glad to," she said. "Just let me know."

Her words made me feel better. I didn't want to tell her that I'd never been in debt before and that a debt worried me to death. So I didn't say anything.

After the snow had melted from the mountain, I grew more despondent. Neither the sight of Jo-Anne nor of Grace could cheer me. My grades went down, and some of the teachers asked me what had happened to me. Everyone around me seemed happy, for April had come again. And Jo-Anne seemed gayer than ever. Several of my teammates had their eyes on her constantly, and it only made me more despondent.

Grace coaxed me again one day to tell her what was wrong. "You always like spring on the mountain," she said.

Then I decided I had to tell somebody my trouble and she

was the one to tell. "Grace," I confessed, "I need money—ten dollars!"

"I don't have it," Grace said quietly. "If I did, you could have it. But that doesn't help. Maybe I'll think of a way. . . ."

I didn't think she would, but it made me feel better—just to share my worry.

On April fifteenth something happened to me that the whole school witnessed. We were gathering for assembly period when Jo-Anne handed my sweater back to me!

"I'm tired of it," she said, without the pretty smile on her lips. "And I'm tired of your ways. You go around with your lower lip drooped as if the world had turned upside down and smashed you. You never have anything to say. You've just become a bore and everybody knows it." She left me standing there with my sweater in my hand.

I was stunned. I couldn't speak. My face grew hot, and I felt everybody looking at me. When I looked up I saw Grace and Roy standing at the other side of the auditorium. They were looking in my direction, and Grace suddenly started to talk to Roy, and neither looked my way again. I don't know how I got through that day at school.

After school I didn't wait for Grace. I hurried out and away from them all. But just as I started up the mountain, Grace overtook me.

"I've thought of something, Shan. I know a way to get ten dollars."

I looked at her without speaking. I was still stunned.

"You know there's a big price at Dave Darby's store for roots and hides and poultry," she said, speaking quickly. "I noticed that sign yesterday. And you know the coves above the gorges are filled with ginseng, yellowroot, and mayapple root."

She waited for me to speak. I walked in silence for a while, thinking it was all too late now—thinking I'd sell my sweater for whatever I could get for it.

"When is the note due?" she asked.

"Ten more days," I said. "April twenty-eighth."

"We'll have it by then," she said.

We, I thought. I looked at her and thought of Jo-Anne. Jo-Anne was pretty and gay and popular, but her face had changed in my mind. I began to wonder if all that gaiety was real—and what she had meant by "love." I was too puzzled to think anything out.

Grace and I walked along silently. We didn't stop at the gorge because Grace had suggested that we go into the cove. I just followed along and started to hunt ginseng after Grace had started.

I never saw anyone before who could find three-prong and four-prong ginseng like Grace. We found patches of yellowroot and mayapple. We filled our lunch pails with these precious roots and I took them home, strung them the way Mom used to string apples and shuckbeans to dry and hung them on nails on the wall above our stove.

We stopped every evening that week and gathered wild roots and I brought them home to dry. On April twenty-seventh, one day before my note was due—and I had already received the notice—I took a small paper sack of dried mayapple roots, a small sack of yellowroot, and more than a pound of the precious ginseng roots to Dave Darby. When he was through weighing the roots he did some figuring. Then he said, "It all comes to sixteen dollars if you trade it out in the store."

"How much if I take cash?" I asked.

"Fifteen dollars," he said.

"Let me have the cash."

I went straight to the Citizens' State Bank and paid off my note. And I had five dollars for Grace. I never felt better, not even when I was so much in love with Jo-Anne.

As I walked home with Grace, I told her how much the roots had brought. "This is not your half," I said as I gave her the five dollars, "but we'll dig more until we get your share. I paid my note."

"Wonderful," she said, smiling at me.

I looked at Grace. Whatever had been wrong with me, I wondered. Why didn't I see before that she had beauty such as Jo-Anne could never have? Grace was as beautiful as our mountain was in April, prettier than a blossom of wild phlox or a mountain daisy. She was as solid as the jutted cliffs, I thought, and as durable as the mountain oaks.

"Now ask me if there is anything more I want from you," I said as I took her arm to help her up the mountain toward the gorge and the wild-root coves.

"What is it?" she asked quickly.

"Take off Roy Tomlinson's sweater," I said. "I'm awfully tired of looking at it."

"But what will I do without it?" she said. "It keeps me warm."

I didn't answer. I started to pull off mine. Then I felt her hand on my arm. "No, Shan," she said. "Keep it awhile. I couldn't wear it yet."

We stood silently on the mountain path and looked at each other. "I couldn't wear it yet," she had said. And that was all the promise I needed. I knew how fine she was, and I was proud that she would not discard Roy Tomlinson's sweater as Jo-Anne had done, without a word to him first.

I didn't know what she was thinking as we started down the

path, and she didn't know what I was thinking. But I didn't ask her, and she didn't ask me.

Jesse Stuart
(Born 1907)

Jesse Stuart, born near Riverton, Kentucky, never strayed far from his roots. Poet, novelist, and short-story writer, he penned some of the most beloved books in American literature—such as *The Thread That Runs So True, Hie to the Hunters, Foretast of Glory,* and *Beyond Dark Hills.*

THE GREEN DRESS

Cathryn Miller

She was still in love with the man she married twenty-seven years before. No, make that more in love. That's why it hurt so, to discover in his art—a rival.

Spring had come late that year. Which may have been why it hit them both so hard. Typical of their relationship, Meredith and Ben had reacted to the season in opposite fashions. With fresh awakenings of a youthful nostalgia, Meredith had fallen in love with her husband all over again. Ben, on the other hand, had fended off her romantic overtures, instead spending all of his free time locked up in the sun room of their hilltop home. Inspired by the very sights and sounds that had stirred his wife's poetic heart, Ben was painting again.

* * *

It was well into May, with tulips and daffodils adding patches of brilliance to their country yard, before Meredith finally dared to venture inside the room to peek at his completed canvases. It was loneliness that pulled her more than curiosity. Ben's artistic temperament had always insisted that she not see his work until he chose to present it. Wary of his quick temper, she had learned early to comply. As she hesitated on the threshold, she reassured herself that twenty-seven years of marriage carried with it some liberties. Anyway, today he was giving a seminar in a neighboring town and would not be back until early evening. How would she ever know?

The thought of Ben's work touched another sore spot as she turned the doorknob. After the uncertainty of many career changes, which had almost cost them Ben's health and their marriage, her husband was finally well established in his own computer consulting business. But his flexible schedule seemed to give them less time together instead of more. Meredith had supported him steadfastly through all of the turmoil of the past fifteen years, but she knew that Ben viewed her own job as book store manager as a reminder of his perceived inadequacies. He had been unable to paint for years. She was relieved when his interest in computers had given him a fresh start, but saddened when the security of employment had not brought more security to their relationship.

The paintings were propped against the baseboards below the windows. From the doorway she could see the soft pastels of the drifting watercolors that were his trademark. But as she walked closer, she noted with surprise that the first pastoral background also included a human figure—something Ben had never painted before. Nature had always been the focus of his work. Many of his scenes were true-to-life renditions of the farm fields or the pine and oak woods near their log home or the meandering river that formed the southern boundary of their property. His work was well regarded by his peers and he had managed to sell several samples. But in all his years of artwork, Benjamin Forrest had never sketched people into his scenes.

As Meredith examined each of his recent pieces, she realized instantly that the same female figure was part of every canvas. Her face was always hidden from view and her hairstyle, even hair color, varied from print to print. But in every scene the pale, spring-green dress that she wore caught the viewer's eye like a beacon.

It was a sleeveless sun dress with wide, tie-back ribbons done in a feminine bow at the small of her back. In some poses, the wind that swept the grasses into undulating waves molded the green dress against her provocative figure. In the forest scenes, a shaft of sunlight caught her among the shadowy evergreens, and her skin seemed to glow beneath it, so that the cloth appeared translucent. Although the girl was never in the foreground and was often only an ethereal suggestion amid springtime greenery,

Ben had managed to make her the center of attention, neverthe-less. Or perhaps it was only to his wife's mistrustful eye that she seemed so seductive.

Meredith envied the slim, youthful figure and gorgeous, long hair, so opposite to her own brown curls and the fifty-one-year-old shape that had widened with the birth of each of her children. When she had complained about how gravity and age were coconspiring against her, Ben had always insisted that she was as attractive as ever. Her bedroom mirror told her otherwise. Although her hair was still a rich chestnut, the skin of her face betrayed her age. Her best friend assured her that the lines that bracketed her mouth and webbed out from the corners of her green eyes were marks of laughter and character and should be borne proudly. But Meredith knew that if she could glimpse the face of the girl in the green dress, her skin would be smooth and flawless.

❧

For a few days Meredith allowed her suspicions to simmer in silence. Was she someone he had recently met and fallen in love with? Or was she a fantasy he had conjured out of his marital boredom? One was almost as bad as the other. Ben still favored her with his kisses and his brown-eyed smile each morning and curved his solid warmth around her every night, but Meredith would not be deceived. She could not remember the last time he had said that he loved her.

Saturday dawned sunny and warm, and the two of them brought their coffee out into the backyard after breakfast. Meredith was poring half-heartedly over her gardening book while Ben read the morning paper when they were both distracted by a familiar sound.

It was the honking of the geese, and they stood and scanned the skies for the welcome sight. Suddenly, there they were, streaming towards them in a trembling, black skein as they tugged spring over the southern horizon.

A rush of joy pounded through her. There was always hope, as eternal as the cycle of the seasons and the return of the geese. Impulsively, Meredith turned to Ben. "Let's take the day off and hike down to the river. I'll make a picnic lunch. We can just relax and dangle our feet and talk. It'll be like old times."

Ben's unshaven face creased in a weak smile of apology. "Sorry, Mer. I planned to paint today. You know what they say . . ."

No, Meredith did not know what "they" said. Make hay while the sun shines? Time's a-wasting? The wife's always the last to know? Which cliché applied? she wondered ruefully.

Her jealousy of the mysterious female who was stealing her husband boiled over. Unable to bite back the words, she confronted him.

"Ben . . . I . . . I looked at your paintings this week. You've never put people in your pictures before. Who . . . who's the girl in the green dress?" Heart hammering, she waited for him to respond, her fear distancing them further. When he turned from her to look down over the fields instead of replying, anxiety churned in her stomach and left a taste like copper in her mouth. That simple motion had confirmed her worst doubts. Tears were beginning to blur her vision of the man she loved with heart and soul, and she wished she had never stepped foot in his studio. When he finally turned to answer her, she was stumbling across the patio, fearful imaginings running rampant through her thoughts. But his quiet response carried across the yard and stabbed her heart before she could close the sliding-glass door between them.

"An old girlfriend, Mer . . . just an old girlfriend."

⁂

Meredith had often used housework as an outlet for frustration and anger. Today she was using it to distract her from panic. She knew that she should have met Ben's statement with a frontal attack, but her bones had turned to water, and her reeling mind had become incapable of coherent argument.

It was the closets that bore the brunt of her frenetic energy. She had finished the cupboards in the boys' bedrooms and was now attacking the one that she shared with Ben. Even though the exodus of her grown sons during the past two years had freed up space in their bedrooms, neither she nor her husband had moved any of their own belongings out of this room. They were content to hang their clothes together, not even bothering to separate items towards his or her sides. She smiled when she recalled her mother's astonishment on learning that even their sock drawer and underwear drawer were coed. Then the thought that she might soon be packing her clothes into suitcases erased the smile with a fresh wave of nauseating fear.

By noon, she had washed down the walls and shelves and had vacuumed the floor of the cramped space, fighting all the while to drive treacherous thoughts away. Clothes and shoes were back in place, and she decided to leave the miscellaneous junk that would go up on the shelves until after lunch.

She stood to stretch her aching back, then sat on the edge of the bed that they might never share again. Thoughts of finality continued to ambush her.

Her gaze rested unwillingly on the framed wedding photograph on her night table. Unable to stop herself, she leaned towards it to lovingly trace the lines of her bridegroom's face and the thick, black hair that had not changed over the years. He was handsome, but then she had dated many attractive men during her teenage years and beyond. For Meredith though, there had been no doubt that Benjamin Forrest was the man with whom she wanted to share the rest of her life. Although he had unmistakable physical appeal and a personality and intelligence that had charmed her, it had been his overwhelming love for her that had swept her off her feet. No man had ever made her feel so wanted, so special. Even in this photograph, their love was an almost tangible presence as they gazed at each other, eyes deep with promise. Tears seeped from beneath clenched lids as Meredith ached for the loss of those emotions. She had always made excuses for the complacency that had replaced the fire, certain that all they needed was time and attention to rekindle it. But if he had truly found someone else . . .

Meredith pressed her fisted palms against her eyes in an effort to stop the tears. It was too unfair! *She* was the romantic, the one who tried to smooth over the rough spots and keep the love alive. *She* was the one who was dissatisfied with a mundane relationship and might have looked for someone else. But had her nagging finally driven Ben to take comfort in someone who would accept him for what he was? What was she going to do if he left her? She blew her nose and told herself that this whole thing might be all in her head. Reason dictated that his nonchalance was surely an indication that this "old girlfriend" was nothing more than a memory. That thought did little to ease her hurt. This ghost had come between them. They would have to face each other eventually and talk frankly, a skill they had not managed to perfect during their years together. Meredith wasn't sure how to handle it, or indeed if she was capable of handling such a discussion at all.

Suddenly her eyes fell upon the stack of old photo albums waiting on the floor, and her breathing quickened. With trembling fingers she retrieved Ben's brown binder from the bottom of the pile and stared at it for a moment as self-righteousness debated with conscience. Curiosity winning over fear, slowly Meredith began to turn the pages.

There had not been a long parade of girlfriends, but Meredith had viewed each female countenance caustically, wondering if it might be *the one*. She was beginning to realize that she had no way of knowing which girl was being painted in miniature in her husband's faceless portraits. She had just made up her mind to halt this foolhardy search when she had found her.

Actually, there were two prints of the same young woman. Her brown hair tumbled loose in waves in one of them and trailed down her back in a thick braid in the second. But the dress was unmistakable. In reality it was more blue than green, closer to an aqua shade in a print of cornflowers and daisies. Meredith recognized the squared neckline that set off the smooth, tanned skin, and the ties that were looped in an old-fashioned bow at the back. There was one of the girl seated in a field on a blanket. An open picnic basket gaped invitingly beside her. . . . In the last frame, she stood atop a sand dune, face turned to the wind that was blowing fog in across the sea, plastering her damp dress to her young figure.

In both pictures, the beautiful girl had worn the dress of Ben's paintings: the garment of his dreams and his imaginings. Meredith knew it well. During that wonderful summer it had been her favorite.

⟡

A tentative knock on the door roused her from her reverie. Ben was standing there, a tender smile on his face. When he walked to sit on the bed beside her, he saw the pages she had been viewing, the girl in the green dress displayed across them.

"Ah . . . I see you've found her. I always loved that dress, Mer. You looked like springtime when you wore it, with your green eyes and wind-blown hair." He took the book from her hands and turned the pages musingly. Then he put it aside and, with a gentle forefinger, angled her face towards his. She wasn't sure whether he could tell she'd been crying, but his kiss didn't feel like paternal comforting. When he pulled back from her, he brushed the hair from her forehead in an intimate gesture.

"I love these green eyes." She blinked to stop fresh tears as he continued, his voice husky. "I fall in love with you all over again every spring, Meredith, and this year was worse than ever. And for some reason I started remembering you in that green dress. . . ."

"Blue," she corrected him. He smiled and kissed her again, longer this time.

"The nostalgia got me painting again. You saw my first attempts at figures. What did you think of them?"

Meredith thought about owning up to her horrible suspicions. She considered confronting him for the umpteenth time about the importance of communication, about her need for *words,* not just the physical signs of love. But instead she smiled at the man that she cherished more than life itself and said, "They're wonderful." Her voice thickened with emotion. "And I love you, I love you, I love you!"

Their next kiss went on for a long, long time.

Cathryn Miller

Cathryn Miller of Sudbury, Ontario, never dreamed that one of her stories, "Delayed Delivery," would be sent around the world by Dr. James Dobson and Focus on the Family in 1994, thus changing her life. A homemaker, mother, teacher, and writer, she pens some of the most memorable stories to come out of Canada today.

A SONG FROM
THE HEART

Mabel McKee

Turned down again! This time her money—and self-confidence—were almost gone. When she asked the reason for the rejection, she was told, "The notes you sing are perfect. But there are many notes missing. These are the notes in your heart."

How could she find those missing notes? She had no idea.

*T*he rusty old car jolted up the hill, down it, and started up another. The engine sputtered noisy protests to the road, so filled with ruts that the driver found it impossible to miss all of them. The lone passenger in the car clenched her hands and tried to keep from crying. Several times she spoke, always asking the same question, "How much farther is it to Heartsease?"

The driver mumbled back his answer, "Not very fur now."

At first he had tried to talk to Jeanne Berthels. When she had climbed into his car, pointed out at the Junction as a taxicab, he had begun asking questions. Her chilliness, however, had soon frozen him into silence.

With each turn of the wheels Jeanne vowed, "I shall never enter a radio studio again. I shall never sing. No one in this town shall know I even know a note of music. I never—"

The car gave another lurch and stopped dead still. Frantically Jeanne clutched the seat. While she straightened her hat and made her position more secure, the old man climbed out of the car and went to look at the motor.

While he examined it, Jeanne snuggled closer in the great Scottish blanket Gordon had given her as a parting present. The events of the last week passed in a long, dreary procession through her mind. She was again singing in a room hung with heavy crimson curtains, singing a medley of southern songs Madame had liked particularly, a number of "blues" songs Madame did not like, but which she felt would interest the manager of the station. At the close of her audition the accompanist had said, "Your voice is rich; your notes are perfect."

After that Jeanne and Gordon had chatted happily together while she waited for the manager's verdict. They were planning for a happy future as friends, planning evenings at lectures, concerts, picnics at the lake, when the warm days of summer should come. The accompanist's words had made Jeanne sure of a contract.

They had hardly noticed the manager's secretary was in the room until she had spoken a few terse sentences; then both had sat speechless. Right now, the secretary had told them, the program at the studio was so full the manager felt he could not add her to their roster of entertainers. Later perhaps he could. The manager would get in touch with her when there was a vacancy.

On the way home Jeanne had been too heartbroken with disappointment to talk. Gordon, however, had raged, "You're too good for them. The manager knew when he heard you sing you'd be too expensive for them. What they're wanting is cheap music. They can't afford you."

Gordon had not known of the other failures, the other stations Jeanne had visited and at which she had sung. He did not know of her songs to the leader of a large choir or the ones she had sung for the manager of the Chautauqua Company. He had been in the South covering a national convention for the paper, for which he was star reporter, when these had occurred.

Jeanne could not tell him about these nor about how little money she had left. Gordon was too successful to have much use for a failure. Jeanne was sure of that. Later that evening, however, she made her way back to the studio and begged for a little talk with the manager.

After she had told him about her other failures, she tossed a heartbroken question at him. "What's wrong with my voice? Madame says my notes are perfect. But I can't get an engagement. What's wrong?"

The manager's bored look suddenly changed to one of interest.

The man leaned forward. "My dear," he said kindly, "the notes you sing are perfect. But there are many notes missing. These are the notes in your heart. Most of our listeners, as you know, are in homes. Evening programs are their favorites. For these they want the kind of music mothers sing to their children in sweet crooning voices with heartbreak, love, and laughter in them. You're too remote, too far away from people for that. Pardon me, but I must tell you that your singing is too mechanical, too much of an attempt to sing perfect notes and not to move people's hearts."

"Come back when you've learned to sing the hidden notes in your heart as beautifully as you do the others, and I'll offer you a salary which will stagger you."

Jeanne Berthels was now far away from the city, sitting in a car while a gruff old man fussed at a dilapidated engine. She was on her way to the home of a small-town physician to be his secretary and companion for his daughter, who spent her days in a wheelchair. Oh, it was a strange position for a musician, but Jeanne, who needed money so badly, had fairly rushed to get it when she heard of a vacancy through an employment agency.

The motor was running now, and they were again jolting down the hilly road. Jeanne was once more murmuring the vow she had made. "Up in this village no one shall even know I have a singing voice."

"That's Heartsease up on that hill just beyond the town." The driver was talking again. "It looks old, but it's not. The old doctor has steam heat and a sun parlor and everything nice for his daughter."

Jeanne looked at the little houses on each side of the crooked street down which they drove, the large consolidated school attended by the children of the workers in the clay plant and the mine who made this town their home. Beyond a pretty little white church building was the doctor's office. The old-fashioned sign hanging from the veranda announced the place.

Heartsease was a rambling, comfortable building with a sign, which was a counterpart of that at the office, hanging from two posts in the front yard. Evergreen trees around the house and hills back of it added to the beauty of the place. Jeanne liked it more and more as she neared it. Here she would start a new life.

Here she would read the novels Gordon would some day write. Gordon could not come to see her. She had told him when she said good-bye that their friendship was over. Better far never to see Gordon again than to let him know she was a complete failure. Tears sprang to her eyes while she lived over again the parting with Gordon.

Inside the physician's home Jeanne had to forget everything, even Gordon, to greet Doctor Beverly, a slender scholarly man in his early fifties, and his daughter, a young girl of seventeen. She reached up a beautiful hand to Jeanne. In a silvery voice filled with delight she exclaimed, "Oh, you're young, too, very young. What wonderful evenings we can have together!"

"Don't ever let Miss Fay know if you feel sorry for her," the old housekeeper told Jeanne when she had shown her to her room. "She thinks life is a happy adventure."

Their dinner was interrupted by a call for the physician, so the two girls were alone when they reentered the living room with its great cases of books, its radio, its pretty pictures, its attractive furnishings. To herself Jeanne thought, *What a wonderful father the doctor is! He's done everything to make this home so lovely and perfect his daughter won't miss walking so much.*

Aloud she said, "You have the loveliest home I've ever lived in."

Fay was radiant. "That's great! Father says it's perfect, but he likes everything I do. What I've needed since I made over this funny house was some one who didn't want to flatter me to tell me it's OK." Her blue eyes grew earnest now. "You see it's intended to be a place where Father can relax and be happy."

Jeanne's hands grew tense. This girl, who lived her days in a wheelchair, had planned this house. It had not been furnished for her, as Jeanne had thought.

After that came the busiest days Jeanne had ever known. Her mornings were spent in the physician's office. Here she learned to give first aid to the wounded, encouragement to the sick of heart. "We must give them cheerfulness and courage even as we give them pills and powders," Doctor Beverly often told her. "These people have troubles. You and I, who have none, just try to help them with their problems."

Weeks had passed before Jeanne saw the physician depressed. He came into the living room with dragging feet one evening. "Sam Dempsey's dead, Fay," he said. "And those seven little children and that sick wife are left to struggle on without him."

Jeanne was the one who coaxed him to the lounge, covered him with a light blanket, and went to the kitchen to bring him hot milk. While she was gone, Fay fussed with the radio, switching from station to station. "I can't get anything but jazz orchestras," she sighed when Jeanne was in the room again.

The doctor disliked jazz orchestras. He liked old-fashioned songs. Now he murmured, "I'd give a fortune if one of them were only singing 'Sun of My Soul' or 'Abide With Me.'"

Jeanne clenched her hands until they hurt. Oh, she could not sing now and bring back all the jagged, tearing heartaches! She told herself this until she noticed that the physician's face was twitching as though with pain. Rising, she walked to the old-fashioned piano. Softly she touched the keys, and still more softly she began to sing one of his favorite songs, "The Long, Long Trail."

She was not singing perfect notes now. They had been forgotten. She was crooning as she sang, not for beauty, but to bring healing to the man who was suffering for the patient he could not cure, the family he could not hold together.

When the song was ended, the physician was asleep. Fay had left the room to meet with the boys of her Americanization class in the big comfortable kitchen, so that her father would not be disturbed. Jeanne joined her there to tell her that her father was resting.

"We were listening to your music," said the girl in the wheelchair with a glorious smile. "And Benito wants you to teach him those songs. He wants to come tomorrow evening for his first lesson."

Two dark pleading eyes looked into Jeanne's brown ones. A youth in broken Italian voiced his own pleas. There seemed nothing Jeanne could do but agree to Fay's plans for the next evening.

***

Jeanne heard the shrill mine whistles in the quiet of the night and sprang from her bed. They told just one fact, an accident at the mine. She dressed and in the hall met the rest of the family, their faces grave and uneasy. "Could you go with me?" Doctor Beverly already had Jeanne's coat. "We'll need all the help we can get if this is a serious accident."

The whistles continued until they were at the mine, around the shaft of which flickered many lights. Jeanne heard with bated breath of the explosion. Forty-seven men were entombed in the mine. The rescue crew was ready to go down.

"Care for the women," the doctor advised Jeanne as he left her to join the rescue crew. "Get them into the superintendent's office and sing to them."

Through that night Jeanne sang to these women songs they loved although they did not understand the words. She sang until some of them dropped to sleep.

Bulletins came from the rescue crew, but these were not brought to the office until one came which said that the imprisoned men had tapped on the roof of their level to the rescue crew working above that they were alive. Hours later came the word that the men had been reached and the first cage of them was coming up.

The waiting women rushed outside with little cries of joy and bursts of laughter. Jeanne followed them.

Suddenly in the crowd she ran face-to-face with Gordon Barnes and an array of other newspaper men. She did not realize that he was beside her, so anxious was she to reach the tipple to see if the doctor was safe and not too tired. Gordon was with her, too, when the cage reached the top, when the men were helped from it, when dark-eyed Benito, weary and weak, was helped from the cage.

The Italian searched the crowd near him until his eyes lighted on Jeanne. He waved his weak hands toward her. "I sing to them," he called. "I sing them the songs you teach me. I sing, and they quit swearing and listen to Pierre say the prayer."

<hr>

Even Benito was in the crowd at the little station when Jeanne left the Junction. Like the old doctor and Fay, he said, "You come back soon. We'll always be looking for you."

The entire week had been a hurried one for Jeanne. At first she had refused to see the manager of the radio station, brought to the little town in the hills by the newspaper stories about her night of song, about Benito's singing to the miners. "I can't go back and sing just to entertain people," she told the doctor. "It's such an idle life. What if I have the missing notes in my heart? They may leave when I'm away from the people who brought them."

"They will never leave," the physician returned. "The life isn't idle. You'll be singing to millions, your heart crying out messages in those songs, messages that will make the sorrowful smile, that will even lead the unbelieving to God."

On the dirty little accommodation train she waved and waved as it steamed and puffed away. She waved until the station became a speck; then she wiped away a few tears and tried to smile. After a time she was the old eager Jeanne again. The conductor had brought her a telegram.

"Leave the train at Brocton," it read. "I'm motoring there to meet you. Stop. The interview I want isn't for my paper but for Gordon Barnes alone. Gordon."

Mabel McKee

Mabel McKee was responsible for some of the most moving inspirational literature of the early twentieth century; today, sadly, little is known about her.

A ROSE FOR
MISS CAROLINE

Arthur Gordon

𝒻or half a year Miss Caroline walled herself off from the town, for the worst possible fate had befallen her— she had been jilted.

Then, mysteriously, every Saturday without fail, an American Beauty rose was delivered at Miss Caroline's door.

*E*very Saturday night, all through that lazy spring, I used to take a rose to Miss Caroline Wellford. Every Saturday night, rain or shine, at exactly eight o'clock.

It was always the best rose in the shop. I would watch Old Man Olsen nest it tenderly in green tissue paper and fern. Then I would take the narrow box and pedal furiously through the quiet streets and deliver the rose to Miss Caroline. In those days, after school and on Saturdays, I worked as delivery boy for Olsen, the florist. The job paid only three dollars a week, but that was a lot for a teenager then.

From the beginning there was something a little strange about those roses—or rather, about the circumstances under which I delivered them. The night the first one was sent I pointed out to Mr. Olsen that he had forgotten the card.

He peered at me through his glasses like a benevolent gnome. "There isn't any card, James." He never called me Jimmy. "And furthermore the—uh—party sending this flower wants it done as quietly as possible. So keep it under your hat, will you?"

I was glad Miss Caroline was getting a flower, because we all felt sorry for her. As everybody in our small town knew, the worst of all fates had befallen Miss Caroline. She had been jilted.

For years she had been as good as engaged to Jeffrey Penniman, one of the ablest young bachelors in town. She had waited while he got himself through medical school. She was still waiting when, halfway through his internship, Dr. Penniman fell in love with a younger, prettier girl and married her.

It was almost a scandal. My mother said that all men were brutes and that Jeffrey Penniman deserved to be horsewhipped. My father said, on the contrary, that it was the right—no, the sacred duty—of every man to marry the prettiest girl who would have him.

The girl Jeffrey Penniman married was a beauty, all right. Her name was Christine Marlowe, and she came from a big city. She must have had an uncomfortable time in our town, because naturally the women despised her and said unkind things about her.

As for poor Caroline, the effect on her was disastrous. For six months she had shut herself up in her house, stopped leading her Girl Scout troop, given up all civic activities. She even refused to play the organ at church anymore.

Miss Caroline wasn't old or unhandsome, but she seemed determined to turn herself into an eccentric old maid. She looked like a ghost that night when I delivered the first rose. "Hello, Jimmy," she said listlessly. When I handed her the box, she looked startled—"For me?"

Again the next Saturday, at exactly the same time, I found myself delivering another rose to Miss Caroline. And the next Saturday yet another. The third time she opened the door so quickly that I knew she must have been waiting. There was a little color in her cheeks now, and her hair no longer looked so straggly.

The morning after my fourth trip to her house, Miss Caroline played the organ again in church. The rose, I saw, was pinned to her blouse. She held her head high; she did not glance once at the pew where Dr. Penniman sat with his beautiful bride. What courage, my mother said, what character!

Week after week I delivered the rose, and gradually Miss Caroline resumed her normal life. There was something proud about her now, something defiant almost—the attitude of a woman who may have suffered an outward defeat, but who knows inwardly that she is still cherished and loved.

The night came, eventually, when I made my final trip to Miss Caroline's house. I said, as I handed her the box, "This is the last time I'll bring this, Miss Caroline. We're moving away next week. But Mr. Olsen says he'll keep sending the flowers."

She hesitated. Then she said, "Come in for a minute, Jimmy."

She led me into her prim sitting room. From the mantel she took a model of a sailing ship, exquisitely carved. "This was my grandfather's," she said. "I'd like you to have it. You've brought me great happiness, Jimmy—you and your roses."

She opened the box, touched the delicate petals. "They say so much, though they are silent. They speak to me of other Saturday nights, happy ones. They tell me that he, too, is lonely. . . ." She bit her lip, as if she had said too much. "You'd better go now, Jimmy. Go!"

Clutching my ship model, I fled to my bicycle. Back at the shop, I did what I had never had the nerve to do. I looked in the file where Mr. Olsen kept his untidy records, and found what I was looking for. "Penniman," it said in Mr. Olsen's crabbed script. "Fifty-two American Beauties—twenty-five cents. Total: thirteen dollars. Paid in advance."

Well, I thought to myself. *Well!*

The years went by, and one day I came again to Olsen's flower shop. Nothing had changed. Old Man Olsen was making a corsage of gardenias, just as he used to do.

We talked awhile, my old boss and I. Then I said, "Whatever became of Miss Caroline? You remember—she got the roses."

"Miss Caroline?" He nodded. "Why, she married George Halsey—owns the drugstore. Fine fellow. They have twins."

"Oh!" I said, a bit surprised. Then I decided to show Mr. Olsen how smart I had been. "D'you suppose," I said, "that Mrs. Penniman ever knew her husband was sending flowers to his old flame?"

Mr. Olsen sighed. "James, you never were very bright. Jeffrey Penniman didn't send them. He never even knew about 'em."

I stared at him. "Who did, then?"

"A lady," said Mr. Olsen. He put the gardenias carefully into a box. "A lady who said *she* wasn't going to sit around watching Miss Caroline make a martyr of herself at *her* expense. Christine Penniman sent those roses."

"Now *there,*" he said, closing the lid with finality, "was a woman for you!"

Arthur Gordon

Arthur Gordon, former editor of *Good Housekeeping* and *Guideposts,* has written a number of books and several hundred memorable short stories. Today, he lives and writes from his native Savannah, Georgia.

THE ATTIC
BRIDE

Margaret E. Sangster, Jr.

Alma Kent and her mother looked at each other despondently. It couldn't be! The millionaire father of the groom was coming after all. It wasn't his kind of a wedding.

What should they do?

For starters, they could go up to the attic.

*A*lma Kent had strained her financial resources to fill her hope chest. To purchase the simple garments in which she would be married was even more of a strain. Her salary as stenographer at the mill was very tiny, and out of that salary she had to pay most of the running expenses of her mother's cottage. As Alma surveyed the aforementioned hope chest, nevertheless, she was delighted with it, for her household linens were quite adequate, she had hemmed the napkins by hand and monogrammed them, and had crocheted the heavy lace that edged the bureau scarfs and pillow slips.

"I don't think any girl ever had prettier things," she told her mother.

"I wish it were in my power, honey, to give you more of prettiness. I'd like to give you dozens and dozens of towels and sheets and tablecloths. I'd like to give you a big wedding, and a satin dress with a train, and a veil of point lace." Alma stifled a sigh. She did not want her dear, self-sacrificing mother to guess that she herself would have enjoyed a big wedding and a satin bridal dress.

"It's much more sensible, Mummy," she said, "for me to be married in a traveling suit. If I do say it who shouldn't, it's the smartest traveling suit in this town, too! There's nothing nicer than blue serge, with a frilly blouse and a smart turban. Then, of course, Terry will give me a beautiful corsage to wear with it."

"I'm so glad," Alma's mother was smiling, "that you're marrying a young man with prospects, darling. Yes, Terry will give you a fine corsage bouquet, probably lilies of the valley and orchids. Your engagement ring is lovely, too, and I'm sure you'll have a sweet wedding ring. Oh, things will be easier, once you are married, Alma. You won't have to scrimp and save as you do now. After all, Terry has a rich father—his father will no doubt do something for him."

"I don't think Terry wants his father to do something for him. It will be so easy for us to get along on his salary, we don't need help. Just the same—" she was closing down the lid of her hope chest, "I'm glad his father isn't coming to the wedding. His father lives in such a big house, and has so many servants, and is used to such luxury that I'd be very self-conscious about having him for a guest at such a simple wedding."

Mrs. Kent drew her daughter close. "I agree with you," she said. "There's nothing snobbish about Terry, and probably his father is just like him, but all the same I'm glad that he can't get to the wedding. It's a strain to prepare an entertainment for an unknown millionaire. Of course," she added, "millionaire or no, his son couldn't find a sweeter girl if he traveled the length and breadth of the country."

Alma kissed her mother and said, "You're prejudiced, that's what's wrong with you!"

The doorbell, ringing, caused an interruption. Alma darted from her mother's side; she fairly flew to answer its clanging summons. It was her fiancé, of course—Terry Hollister, lately imported from a distant city to be superintendent of the mill in which Alma had always worked. Alma, peering back over the progress of her romance, felt that she was a Cinderella, for she had liked Terry's looks on the first day when he came to the mill. To her he had embodied the characteristics of a prince charming; he was rich, successful, handsome. She had not dreamed that he would notice her in her corner among the filing cabinets, but he did notice her immediately when he came into the stenographers' room. Before a week he had secured an introduction to her. In less than two weeks he was calling at the cottage and praising her mother's waffles.

"This is like home," he said on the occasion of his initial Sunday supper with the Kents. "At least," he amended, "it's like I always thought home would be. You see, Father and I haven't a home in the sense that yours is a home. Mother died when I was a young-ster, and Father and I have camped out, ever since, in a big house surrounded by butlers. Dad's swell, but he's forgotten what it is to be cozy."

"Your father must be very wealthy," Alma had said.

"He is," Terry told her, "but don't you be envious of him. He hasn't anywhere near what you have, and now that I've left home he's probably the lonesomest man in the world."

<hr />

Yes, in two weeks Terry Hollister was calling at the Kent cottage. In three weeks he was there every evening, and in four weeks—when sitting on the tiny porch in the moonlight—he suddenly reached over and took Alma's hand in his own.

"I love you," he said without preamble, "I love you very much, Alma; will you marry me?"

Alma had been loving Terry since the very beginning, practi-cally since the day of his coming to the mill; but she had not believed he would ever care for her, even though his attentions had been so marked.

"Oh, Terry," she gasped, "indeed, I do care for you!"

They planned to be married as soon as she could "get ready." Getting ready meant filling her hope chest and saving enough money, out of her meager wages, for a trousseau. Terry did not know that. She did not want him to know, either.

Well, they had managed! They had saved on meals and on lights and their few wee luxuries. They had scrimped and sacrificed. Mrs. Kent had made cakes for the neighbors, and Alma had made candy for the woman's exchange. Laboriously they had gathered together enough money to purchase the trim blue serge suit and the hat that went with it, and the frilly blouse. They had remodeled Alma's one evening frock, and they had retrimmed her last spring's party dress. A new fur collar had been added to her street coat.

Now on the eve of her marriage, Alma had good reason to be pleased. As she flew into Terry's arms she was quite satisfied with the plans and preparations.

"Oh, darling," she exclaimed, "we're ready for the wedding tomorrow. I mean my clothes, the house and all. Mother has baked a wedding cake with her own hands, and we're going to have chicken salad and beaten biscuit."

"We're going to have more than that," said Terry, with his arms tight around her, "we're going to have a surprise guest. You can't guess! You know my father was involved in a big business deal and I didn't think he could get away, but I just had a wire to tell me that the deal is finished. Dad's leaving at this moment from the airport in our home city; he's going to fly all night to get here in time for the wedding. What do you think of that? I'll be as proud as punch to have him meet the most marvelous girl in the world and be among those present at our beautiful wedding."

Alma was drawn back in her fiancé's arms and was looking up into his face. "Oh, but Terry," she exclaimed, "I didn't have any idea your father could make it."

"Nor have I," laughed Terry, "and that's why I'm so tickled to death to know he's coming. Aren't you pleased, honey? It's the one thing we needed to make our wedding complete."

"Yes, I am pleased, Terry," Alma answered, and though she managed to smile, she had to wink hard to keep back the tears. Her air castles seemed to be tumbling into dust about her feet.

That night, after Terry had gone home, Alma and her mother held a hurried consultation. Alma was frankly crying now. She had kept up through the evening; she had laughed and joked, but now that Terry had gone, the reaction set in.

"Oh, Mummy," she sobbed, "I simply can't have the kind of wedding we had planned. I mean, you'd like me in a plain blue serge suit that cost—" she gulped, "nine twenty-five; and Terry would never see the cheapness of it because he's in love with me. But with his father here—and rich, and critical—Oh," she gulped back the tide of her emotion, "if only I had a white wedding dress and a veil. If only—"

"It's too late now, I'm afraid, darling. If we'd had a week or two in which to plan, we might have managed, but tomorrow's too soon. We can't manage a different sort of wedding, now. Unless—," she laughed ruefully, "you want me to go up in the attic and get out my wedding dress and veil. They're in a box, under the rafters." She had said it as a joke, had Mrs. Kent, but even as she was speaking Alma's eyes had grown wide and luminous.

"Oh, Mummy," she exclaimed, "why didn't we think of that before! Your wedding dress won't be very far from the fashion of today; really we're wearing the same leg-o'-mutton sleeves, and the same bias skirts, and even the same materials. There's that picture of you in the album downstairs—it might have been made yesterday—we were laughing about it just a tiny while ago. Why, that wedding dress is exactly like the dresses they are showing in the nicest shops downtown. Let's get it out and see if it comes anywhere near fitting!"

Together the mother and daughter, one as light of foot as the other, ran up the narrow stairs to the small attic. Though it was late they pulled and tugged until they had brought forward an old trunk. They delved into it and found the flat pasteboard box that held Mrs. Kent's own bridal finery. They carried the box, in triumph, from the attic and opened it on Alma's bed. There, before them, lay a quaint, puffy-sleeved dress of ivory taffeta and a wide tulle veil, slightly yellowed with the passing of years, and a pair of white kid slippers.

Alma lifted the dress from the box as quick as a flash and held it against her body. Yes, it was the right length and probably it would not be far wrong in width, either. She was quickly out of her dress and her mother was adjusting the taffeta folds.

Oh, the dress was wrinkled and mussed and showed signs of having been laid away for many a long year; but it was still lovely and a hot iron would do wonders. What if it were a trifle wide through the shoulders, a clever tuck or two would simplify matters! What if it were a bit snug around the waist, a seam could be ripped in a crucial point! Mrs. Kent, surveying her daughter, said:

"You look adorable, honey. We'll get at that frock the first thing in the morning. And when Mr. Hollister sees you, he'll think his son's bride is the loveliest bride in the world!"

The Kent cottage was hurry and bustle all through the morning hours. Much stitching and pressing was to be done, as well as the frosting of cakes and the mixing of salad dressing. The guests were to be some of Terry's friends, a few of Alma's intimates, and a baker's dozen of her mother's old friends.

The plain cottage was transformed by mid-afternoon, the time set for the wedding, and when Alma herself stood in front of the mirror and looked at a glimmering reflection, she felt, without any sense of conceit, that she fitted against the cottage's charming background. Her mother, watching misty-eyed, gave a wee sob and turned away.

"You look precious, my darling," she said, before she hurried down to greet the arriving guests.

Terry was the first to come, of course. He and the distinguished gray-haired man who was his father. Terry asked joyously, "Where's Alma?"

Mrs. Kent warned him off with a slim, upraised hand. "It's bad luck," she told him, "to see your bride before the ceremony."

"From what Terry tells me, it's good luck to see this bride any time, Mrs. Kent."

Alma's mother, raising her eyes to his face, thought that he looked more like a benevolent benefactor than a critical millionaire.

***

One of Alma's friends played the wedding march on the parlor organ. The minister took his place before the improvised altar.

When Alma came softly into the room, she was beautiful. The dress she wore had justified her faith in it; it was old-fashioned enough to be smart, and yet it was quaint also. Something in the very age of the taffeta made it mellow and extraordinarily lovely. Terry started forward as he saw Alma standing in the doorway, a rustle ran through the gathering of mutual friends, and the tears stood upon Mrs. Kent's cheeks. Mr. Hollister, Terry's father, spoke aloud.

"Why," he said, "why, my dear child," and before the marriage ceremony could begin, while the wedding march was still playing softly, he stepped forward to kiss his prospective daughter upon one of her round, flushed cheeks. "My dear child," he said again huskily, and then the sweet, solemn ceremony started.

❦

All was excitement and confusion after the minister had pronounced Terry and Alma man and wife. Kissing and handshaking and the throwing of her bouquet followed. Terry's corsage had been kept for the blue traveling suit. A hastily improvised bouquet of white lilies of the valley had been the one that the bride carried with her quaint frock.

The chicken salad had been eaten and the beaten biscuit, and the delicious cool fruit drink that Mrs. Kent had prepared. The wedding cake had been cut amid cheers and impromptu speeches. Not until Alma had run upstairs to change into her traveling suit had Mr. Hollister and Mrs. Kent found a moment in which they could converse. The young people had formed groups, but the father and the mother were in a small oasis in a corner.

"I'm going to be very frank with you, Mrs. Kent," Mr. Hollister began. "I had my doubts about the sort of girl my son would choose, considering that he chose so hastily. I'm one—" he smiled, "who believes in due consideration; although I must confess that my own marriage was the result of love at first sight and my own wedding came pretty quickly. However," he sighed, "I'm getting away from the point. I meant all the time to come to Terry's wedding, but I didn't tell him until the last minute so that I could keep you—I'm ashamed to admit this—and your daughter unawares. Terry had told me he was marrying, you'll pardon me, a poor girl. I wanted to see whether you'd make any attempt at pretense and sham because I was coming. If you had, I would have known. I can see pretense a mile off! Well, I was wrong. Everything was as sweet and simple as if you and Terry and your daughter had been here alone. I'm telling you this because I'm ashamed of myself and I want to apologize. Will you accept my apology?"

"Indeed, I do!" Mrs. Kent laid her hand in Mr. Hollister's large one. "And now I'll make my confession. We are poor and we did, in a way, feel that we were being tested. Alma hadn't even a wedding dress until last night, Mr. Hollister. When we heard that you were coming we rummaged through the attic and produced the one she was wearing. I wore it myself—twenty-one years ago!"

"I like you—and I love your daughter. What can I do for her—and for you—to show how I feel? I thought about buying the young people a home, or giving Alma a bank account of her own, or bonds."

"Don't do that," Mrs. Kent spoke swiftly. "Let them work out their own salvation. I know how Terry and my daughter feel about it. They feel that Terry's making enough money for a young chap—and Alma mustn't be spoiled."

"I don't think that your daughter could be spoiled, but I'll wait. Some day when there are children—"

A burst of laughter interrupted the conversation, and Alma, pretty as a fashion plate in her blue serge and orchids, came running down the stairs.

"This is the first time in years," said the millionaire who stood beside Mrs. Kent, "that I haven't felt lonely."

Margaret E. Sangster, Jr.
(1894–1981)

Margaret E. Sangster, Jr. was born in Brooklyn, New York. An editor, scriptwriter, journalist, short-story writer, and novelist, she was one of the best known and most loved inspirational writers of the early part of the twentieth century.

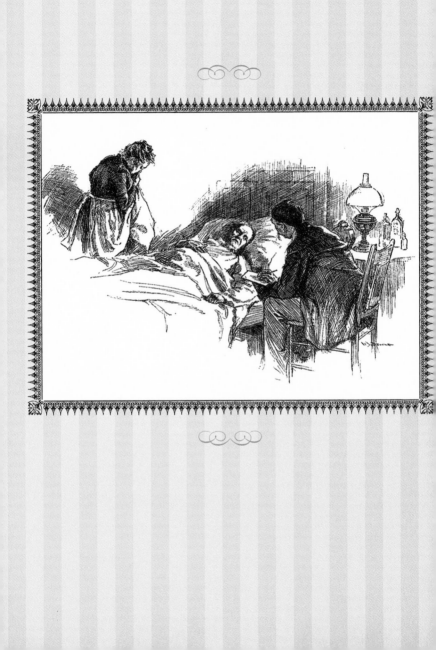

THE LIGHT
OF MY EYE

Wang Yang

Only once in a very long time do I read a story that is so powerful it is virtually impossible to forget. This is one of them. It is about an arranged marriage—and the unexpected love that enters it after the long years.

I was awake as Dr. Chou Taohsiang operated to give me a corneal transplant. They had deadened the nerves around the eye, but I could hear metallic instruments clanking and Dr. Chou speaking.

My right eye had been inflamed and swollen for more than three years. When I checked into Taiwan's Tri-Service General Hospital in Taipei, I could hardly see out of it, and my left eye was severely hyperopic. Doctors discovered that I was suffering from keratitis (inflammation of the cornea).

"You could have picked it up from towels, or from swimming pools," I was told.

"I'm a swimming instructor at an army officers' school," I said.

"That's probably how you caught it," the doctor said.

About a year later, I learned that a corneal transplant could restore sight to my now blind right eye. When I told my wife, she brought out her savings deposit book. She had managed to save some $500 after years of hard work.

"If this isn't enough, we'll try to get more," she said, adding: "You're not like me. An illiterate person is blind though he can see. A man who can read needs both eyes."

I put myself on Dr. Chou's waiting list. A month later, he phoned me. "A driver was involved in a bad car accident," he said. "Before he died, he told his wife to sell parts of his body to help support their children. Could you spare $250?"

The operation and hospital expenses would come to a further $200. I agreed, and was told to check into hospital the following day. I was extremely lucky. People waited for years before a cornea became available, and I told my wife how grateful I was to her for making the operation possible.

As I was being wheeled out of the operating room, my

daughter Yung put her lips close to my ear and said, "Everything went well. Mother wanted to come, but she was afraid."

"Tell her not to come," I said. "But tell her I'm all right. She is not to worry."

———

I was nineteen when I married on my parents' orders.★ My father and my wife's father were close friends and had pledged that if their wives gave birth to a boy and a girl, the children should be married.

I had never set eyes on the girl who was to be my wife until the day she was carried to our house in a bridal sedan chair. After bowing to heaven and earth, she was led to my bedroom. When at last I lifted the red brocade of her bridal headdress, I gasped with horror. Her face was cruelly covered with pockmarks, her nose was a deformity, and beneath sparse eyebrows, her scarred eyelids made her eyes seem swollen. She was nineteen, and looked forty.

I fled to my mother's room and cried all night. My mother told me that I must accept my fate. Homely girls bring good luck; pretty ones court sorrow. But nothing she said reduced my anguish. I would not share a room with my wife, and I did not speak to her. I lodged at school. When summer vacation came, I refused to come home until my father sent a cousin to fetch me.

My wife was cooking supper when I arrived, and raised her head in a smile when she saw me. I walked right past her. After supper, my mother said to me privately, "Son, you are being very cruel. Her face is unattractive, but she does not have an ugly heart."

"No, it must be beautiful," I stormed. "Otherwise how could you have made me marry her?"

My mother's face grew pale. "She is an extremely good girl, understanding and considerate," she said. "She has been in this house more than six months now, and works from morning to night in the kitchen and at the mill. She has not uttered a word of complaint about the way you have treated her. I have not seen her shed a tear. But she is shedding them inside. Do you want her to live like a widow although she has a husband? Put yourself in her place."

My wife and I began to share the same bedroom, but nothing changed the way I felt. She always kept her face down and spoke softly. If I argued with her, she would raise her head to give me a submissive smile, then quickly lower it again. *She's like a ball of cotton wool,* I thought. *No will, no temper.*

In the thirty years of marriage that followed, I seldom smiled at my wife and never went out in her company. Indeed, I often wished her dead.

And yet, my wife proved to be endowed with more patience and love than anyone I know. When we first came to Taiwan, I held a low rank in the army, and my income was barely enough to pay for rent and food. The baby was often ill, and we had to cope with medical expenses as well. When my wife was not looking after the household, she wove straw hats and mats to earn a little money. When we moved to a fishing harbor in the east, she darned fishing nets and, when we moved north, she learned to paint designs on pottery. We never lived in army quarters because the truth was we both feared her meeting people I knew. I was often away from home, but I knew that I needn't worry about our two children or the household, with her looking after everything.

After the operation, my daughter Yung brought me a transistor radio to occupy the long hours while the bandages remained on my eyes. But I had plenty of time to think, and my thoughts kept returning to my wife. I was somewhat ashamed for telling her not to come to see me.

After two weeks, I learned that the stitches would soon be removed. I could not contain my happiness. "When I recover," I told Yung, "I want to pay a visit to the grave of the man who gave me his cornea."

But I was nervous, for I knew there was a chance that the transplant would not take. When they removed the bandage from my right eye, I scarcely dared open it.

"Do you see any light?" Dr. Chou asked.

I blinked. "Yes, from above."

"Yes, that's the lamp," he said, and patted me on the shoulder. "It's a success. You can go home a week from today."

During that week, he tested my eye every day. First I could see shadows, then the number of fingers on his hand. On the day I was going home, I could see the window, the bed, and even the teacups on the table.

"Mother's making your favorite dishes to welcome you home," Yung said when she came for me.

"She's a good wife and a good mother," I replied, words I would never say before.

Yung and I climbed into a taxi. She was strangely silent all the way home. As I walked into the house, my wife was coming from the kitchen with a plate of food. When she saw me, she lowered her head immediately. "You're back," she murmured.

"Thank you for letting me see," I said. It was the first time I remembered ever thanking her for anything.

She walked past me abruptly and put the food on the table. Leaning against the wall with her back toward me, she began to sob. "It is enough to hear you say this. I have not lived in vain."

Yung burst into the room in tears. "Tell him!" she cried. "Let father know you gave the cornea for his eye!" She shook her mother. "Tell him!"

"I only did what I should," my wife said.

I grabbed her by the shoulders, and looked closely at her face. Her left iris was opaque, as my right one had been.

"Golden Flower!" It was the first time I spoke her name. "Why . . . why did you do it?" I demanded, shaking her hard.

"Because . . . you are my husband," she said, burying her head in my shoulder. I held her tight. Then I got down and knelt at her feet.

The writer was raised in the days of arranged marriages when children had to obey parents' orders implicitly.

WHEN LOVE AND
DUTY MEET

Carmie Nesmith

This was a most important evening for Dr. Arnold—
was not Annie to give her answer after the dinner
tonight? But his competition, Southworth, would be
there, too!

And now, this urgent request to attend a sick child
in the tenement district. Surely, after all these years of
devotion to duty, he deserved this one night off!

What was he to do?

*Y*es, keep up your tonic. Certainly, have the prescription renewed if necessary. Oh, yes, I hope you will have no further trouble, but if you do, come again Wednesday. Goodnight."

Then while his patient paused on the threshold, groping for more questions to ask, Dr. Willis Arnold softly but firmly closed the door between them.

"If anyone comes this evening, James," he said to the office boy, "remember I am not at home."

"Yes, sir, I understand," the discriminating James smiled knowingly.

Dr. Arnold bounded up the broad staircase three steps at a time. He entered his room and turned the key in the lock. He pulled out his evening clothes and arranged them with the rapidity and precision of a perfectly adjusted machine. Then he snapped the buttons of his dress shirt in place, and hurrying to the wash bowl began to wash his hands.

It was no wonder he was absent-minded, he told himself; for what the future held in store for him, at least whether it held his heart's desire, would be decided before midnight; for Annie had promised to give her answer at Edith's dinner.

Edith, like all happy young matrons was something of a match-maker, but he found it easy to forgive her. He even suspected her of having planned this particular dinner on his account. She hinted that there would be something quite informal and unusual afterward, evidently just the opportunity he desired. Why then had she invited Southworth too? She must know as well as he that Southworth was no mean rival; that he was richer, younger, more adaptable than himself, and Annie had not found it easy to choose between them.

The ringing of the doorbell broke in upon his reverie. He

softly turned the key in the lock and opened his door in time to hear James's suave voice saying; "No, sir, Dr. Arnold is out on a very important case, sir."

He had just adjusted his white lawn tie exactly to his liking, when the third ring came, a faint, hesitating one, as if the ringer hardly dared make himself known. This time the doctor stepped to the top of the stairs. James had opened the door a scant six inches; his back was uncompromisingly straight.

"No, the doctor's out."

"Could I wait in the hall till he comes?" The voice—a man's voice—was hesitating and apologetic, like the ring. "I want to see him bad, as soon as he comes—my little feller's worse—he's crying enough to break your heart. Dr. Arnold was there this morning and said how if he didn't get better we was to let 'im know. He said if he got worse, he'd hev to go to the hospital an' hev an operation."

Dr. Arnold understood. He had seen a sick child that morning in the tenement district and had prepared the mother for the probable outcome. He stared impulsively down the stairs.

"Come in!" he commanded. The door swung suddenly wide. The man looked at him in a dazed way, but obeyed. He was thinly clad and was shivering with cold, or nervousness, or both.

"Why didn't you let me know before?" the doctor asked.

"I just got home from work. His mother didn't dast leave 'im and she hadn't nobody to send; the others are too little, you know."

"If you had sent me word this afternoon . . ."

He looked at his watch; there was a scant five minutes that he might use and still keep his engagement.

"I'll tell you what I'll do. I'll call up St. Michael's and have an ambulance sent. The house surgeon there will look after him alright."

He strode into his office and took down the receiver of his telephone, the father shambling after.

"Give me 408 Fairview, Central, as quick as you can."

There was something compelling about the low insistent tone. Even Central felt its power; the connecting click was almost instantaneous.

"Is this 408 Fairview? St. Michael's? Can you send an ambulance out for a child at once, probably a surgical case? No? Both ambulances out? That's too bad! You're sure you couldn't get him tonight? Not till tomorrow morning? That won't do. Good-bye."

Then the doctor referred hurriedly to his telephone directory and called up another hospital. The wards were full; there would be a vacancy later. He called up a third. Their surgeon had been called out of town. Again he looked at his watch. His five minutes stretched to ten, but he would make one more effort. He rang up the office of a rising young surgeon of his acquaintance. He was not in, and would not be until ten o'clock. He hung up the receiver with a jerk.

"I'm sorry, my man," he said, dropping into a chair, "but I don't see what more I can do for you. You will have to find another doctor for yourself." The man raised his eyes; they were round and blue like a child's—in fact, when they met Dr. Arnold's, he thought how much like a child's, a sick child's, they were and gave the doctor the long appealing look of a hurt animal.

They faced each other until the silence weighed on them both; then almost inaudibly, his tone showing how useless he felt it was to make the request, the father faltered, "You don't—I don't suppose you would feel you could go yourself, Sir?"

"Impossible."

Suddenly the man's face lighted. "I'll pay you, sir; you needn't be afraid." He pulled a dirty bill from his pocket and eagerly held it out. "Not all at once, of course, I couldn't, Sir. But I'll come here every Saturday night before I go home, as God is my judge I will—I'll pay every cent I owe, if I go hungry to do it."

"No, no, you don't understand, I don't want your money."

He did not understand! He only knew that his last hope had failed. A vision of Edith's dinner table came to the doctor, with the glitter of a vision of china and glass and heaped-up fragrant roses. He saw the white shoulders of Anna Wingates above the filmy form of her gown, her Madonna face, and the look he loved in the serious blue-gray eyes. He saw, too, a second and more distinct vision, a shining cloud, and out of it the strains of wedding music, and Anna in floating bridal robes, his wife.

I promised her I would be there and if I am not, Southworth will be. Who can tell how it might influence her answer? It has been Duty, Duty, Duty—nothing but duty for ten years. Tonight it is love—what is this tenement-house child to me that I should hazard all my future happiness for him? Probably they can find someone else. If they cannot, after all, what does it matter? They have other children, more than they can take care of, and the best the little chap can do for himself or for them is to die.

"No," he said aloud, "you will have to get someone else; I will not go." The father poked the crown of his old hat into shape, turning it around in his hands as if studying its every dent, and at last started to put it on, but remembering himself, lowered it again and moved toward the door. With his hand on the knob, he stopped.

"Goodnight, doctor, only it's hard to give him up; he is our oldest fellow, always telling Ellen how he will take care of her when he gets to be a man. I don't know how she will stand it." The words ended in a low choking sob. He opened the door and it closed heavily behind him.

It is a strange thing, that which for lack of a better name we call the "human heart." The man had no hope of changing the surgeon's decision by this last fervid outburst. Dr. Arnold himself had not thought of yielding to it, but in some way the quivering, anguish-swept note of the one stirred the answering chords in the other. Call it overruling Providence or happy chance, some power there was within or without that brought Dr. Arnold to the door.

"Wait a minute." The laborer had reached the bottom step but turned to find the doctor standing in the broad beam of the flashing chandelier. A minute later he came down the steps, muffled in his heavy coat and carrying his surgical case in his hand. It was January and the still air was stirred with cold. The stars shone in countless points and the streetlight made rainbows in the clouds. The carriage was waiting to take him to Edith's dinner. He motioned the man to get in.

"No, thank you, sir. I'll ride outside." He climbed to the driver's seat, turning up his ragged collar to his ears. Dr. Arnold gave the street and number. The coachman turned the horses' heads. They rattled away.

It was a little after eight o'clock when they reached East Nineteenth Street and stopped before a long row of tenement houses. They paused at the top of the third floor, and a long moaning cry reached their ears.

The room that had seemed only a common place in the morning took on strange uncanny shadows at night. The only illumination came from a small kerosene lamp, and this, like the light in a picture, was concentrated on the central figure of the little sufferer on the bed. By his side knelt the mother, her head buried in the blanket, while in the deeper shadows beyond was another figure that rose as they entered and slipped into the adjoining room.

It was midnight when Dr. Arnold pulled on his coat and turned toward the inner room to speak a word of encouragement to the mother. As he softly opened the door, he heard a voice that clutched his very heart. Could he mistake the voice? The two women, for there were two sitting there in the darkness, turned eager, anxious faces, and in the flickering beam that fell upon them he saw that he was not mistaken: The voice was Annie Wingates's.

"Why are you here?" he asked as soon as he had satisfied the mother.

"Ellen sent for me. She lived with us five years before she was married, she always comes to us when she is in trouble."

He wondered if his hand would have been so steady had he known that she was sitting there. He only said, "Come, you are not needed longer—I will take you home."

As they stepped into the hall, they almost stumbled over the father, stretched out like a watchdog in front of the door. He staggered to his feet.

"Doctor?" he said and stopped. There was an agony of apprehension in the one word.

"Everything is going well."

"God bless you for coming, Doctor. God bless you!"

Dr. Arnold drew Annie's hand through his arm and tenderly guided her down the rickety stairs. Neither spoke until they stepped out under the wintry sky. Then she gave a sigh of relief. "What a nightmare!"

"It is terrible, but remember this is not the part of my life I want you to share. Still, I cannot help being glad you had this little glimpse of it, for it is a very important part; it must be, dear, if it could keep me away from you."

"Oh, it wasn't *that!* I was so afraid—" She stopped.

"Afraid? Afraid of what?"

"That you *wouldn't* come. I knew that if you did not, I could never, never forgive you as long as I lived."

The long, strong fingers closed over the hand on his arm. They both knew that the question was answered.

ROSES

Author Unknown

*C*ynthia, being beautiful, had always had everything: Other girls had to accept her cast-offs. Over time, this supremacy inevitably had its effects on her—and not for the better.

And then came the terrible epidemic.

*A*small town, as small towns will, had humbled itself at the feet of a girl. Her name was Cynthia Reynolds, and she lived with her Aunt Lucinda in a tiny cottage set down in a mass of roses. Roses of every color and shade, large velvety blooms, and tiny clustering ones. They clambered all over the little house, and nodded at Cynthia through her bedroom window in the morning. They kissed over the walk to the house and blossomed thick, interwinding, over the rose arbor. And every once in a while Cynthia gathered the failed petals, saving big tubs of them, and made them into delicate, fragrant rose beads.

Like one of her perfect blossoms, Cynthia grew among her roses. In childhood and in girlhood, it was into her lap that they continued to heap their gifts and adoration; Cynthia took it as a matter of course. She had grown up with beauty and Aunt Lucinda had managed to keep her unspoiled; she never made the mistake of telling her that she was beautiful, but she faced the problem in her own tactful way.

"You are like one of your roses, Cynthia," she would say as she brushed the girl's soft golden curls. "God has to make some of us strong, weather-beaten, and serviceable, and others, like the birds and flowers, for beauty. But the beautiful, too, have their duties to the world, and those who can spread gladness and beauty, shouldn't spoil it with thorns."

And Cynthia would hug her aunt, and perhaps laughing, respond, "Are you afraid I'll develop thorns, Auntie?"

But in time, it became evident that Cynthia was developing thorns. They were threatening thorns that pricked and then couldn't be found. One would never have thought of accusing Cynthia of being selfish, and yet—Aunt Lucinda noticed it first in her beau. As young people will in a small town, they had begun to pair off, but Cynthia never had a "steady." She was always showered with invitations, and after she selected her escort, the other girls were taken as second choice.

Once Aunt Lucinda attempted to remonstrate. "Do you think you ought to go to the dance with Howard, Cynthia? You know he always goes with Ellen, and they really think a lot of each other."

Cynthia looked at her aunt roguishly.

"Do you think we ever value anything we have to take as second choice when we can't get exactly what we want, Auntie?"

Howard's honk sounded in front, and Cynthia flung the words over her shoulder as she ran out.

"Oh, I might, but I don't want to. Why should I?"

Then one day came David Gare. David—nicer than the rest, handsomer, more wonderful. He wandered into her garden from his garden next door. It was June and David first saw her by the arbor with roses all around her, their perfume heavy and alluring. All through the summer he came. They cared for the bushes together, and took huge bouquets to the hospitals and sick people. One evening they sat resting in the garden. David was serious, and Cynthia jokingly prepared him for his funeral, piling roses on his head, hanging them on his ears, and in the lapel of his coat.

He shook them off, and drew her down beside him.

"Cynthia, may I have the most perfect flower in the garden?"

Cynthia chose to misunderstand him. "Of course, David. You may have any and all you want."

"Please take me seriously, Cynthia. It's you I want. I love you, dear. Will you marry me?"

"Oh, David!"

"I'm working up a good practice here, Cynthia. I'll probably never be rich or famous, a small-town doctor seldom is, but we both know and love the people here, and a life of service is, after all, the happiest."

Cynthia was silent for a moment. "You make me feel so selfish, David, but I can't. It would be so hum-drum, and—it sounds worse to say it than when I think it—but I don't want to give up the other boys. I want to travel a bit, and have some more fun before I settle down." So she sent him away as she had sent others before him, with a bit of regret for the days that were gone, but eager for adventure. Only this time it was different; other men seemed so prosaic beside David. And he made it so hard, because he stopped coming to see her entirely. His practice was beginning to demand more of his time, and when he wasn't busy, he was studying.

The last week of August the town was gala with the bright colors of a carnival. Flower-decked floats paraded the streets, and old and young entered into the holiday spirit.

Then in a moment, it seemed a chill settled over the gaiety. Disease had crept among them, and like an octopus with many deadly tendrils, reached out in all directions.

Aunt Lucinda secretly chided herself for having had misgivings regarding Cynthia as she watched her work untiringly among the sick, sometimes at the side of David Gare, hopelessly watching the life go out of a victim or feeding the spark of life and sharing his exaltations when they felt death was defeated, but Aunt Lucinda also felt many a pang of fear at the horrible chances they were taking.

At last the inevitable happened, for with their lowered vitality, David and Cynthia fell ill. There were weeks and weeks of patient fearful watching—weeks of waiting and horrible suspense. And it was over. From David's home came the report that the danger was past. He was very weak, and it would be some time before he would be able to leave the home, but he had fought the fight and won. This news brought to Cynthia's bedside, gave her strength to fight her fight to recovery. And to Cynthia recovery now meant only one thing—David.

But Aunt Lucinda felt a helpless despair as Cynthia gained strength and looked forward to being up and around.

"But, Doctor, you don't mean—you can't mean that her face will always be this way?" she pleaded.

"Why, yes, Miss Lucinda, I'm afraid so."

"You mean her beauty always gone—oh, no, Doctor. It can't be true. Her beauty will all come back to her as her health improves surely, surely?"

"No, Miss Lucinda," said the doctor gently. "Good eating may fill out the hollows in her cheeks, and her complexion clear and color up as her blood improves, but I'm afraid there is no hope that the little red splotches and other blemishes will ever disappear. I'm sorry, Lucinda."

Cynthia herself was too stunned at first to really understand. When first she glanced in the mirror, she fell back as if struck.

"Aunt Lucy, Aunt Lucy—tell me if it isn't me, it can't be me." Aunt Lucinda tenderly stroked her hair. If it seemed as death to Cynthia, it was torture to Lucinda, and often death is kinder than torture.

"You are still beautiful to us, who love you, Cynthia darling," she said. "The real you is just the same, like the fragrance of the roses in the beads."

"Oh, but Aunt Lucy, to have people pity me. To have them see me like this! I'd rather die! I wouldn't mind so much if it had left me homely, but I'm ugly! It won't last, though, will it? When I get stronger they'll go away, surely they will."

Aunt Lucinda let her hope that, as she gained strength, her skin would clear, but Cynthia was convinced that it wouldn't ever be so. She had seen no one but the family doctor and Aunt Lucinda, and she shrank pitifully from the thought of seeing others. David Gare had been away after his illness and her bitterest thought was that sometime, he would have to see her. It seemed the irony of fate that her skin was soft and velvety as ever to the touch, and only in appearance splotchy and ugly. Then one day there came a box of roses with a simple card. "David Gare." Cynthia crushed the roses to her, and Aunt Lucy's heart was broken.

Winter passed. Cynthia tried to fill the empty days with books and household tasks and the garden—when she was sure no one would see her. She could not bring herself, even yet, to face people's eyes.

It was the last of June, and Cynthia was wandering in her garden toward the rose arbor. Memories came flocking to mock her. An early rose, pale and half-blown in a group of lovely buds, dropped a petal as she passed. Cynthia cupped her hand around it in sudden pity. "You're ugly and faded too, aren't you, and when your beauty is gone, there is nothing left. Yes—you still have your fragrance for the rose beads, but I don't even have that— nothing beautiful to make people love and want me now. They only pity me."

She heard a light step on the path, and turned to see Aunt Lucinda with an envelope in her hand.

"David is at the front gate, dear, and sends you this note. He is waiting for an answer."

Cynthia trembled. "Read it to me, Aunt Lucy."

"Oh, not—" and then seeing that Cynthia couldn't, she opened the envelope. "He says, 'Dear Cynthia: May I talk to you for a few moments? I know you have seen no one since you were ill, and you dismissed me once, but I promise not to overstep my bounds if you'll only let me come. I love you, Cynthia. David.'"

"Oh, Aunt Lucy, I can't let him see me. I don't dare! I'd rather he'd remember me always as I was. He—I—oh—oh, I want him so. Tell him 'yes,' Aunt Lucy."

And Aunt Lucy went with blinding tears, stumbling back to David Gare.

At the rose arbor Cynthia waited. She half turned to call her aunt back, but she couldn't speak. The roses that nodded to her from all sides seemed to mock her with their perfection. How often David had compared her to them, giving her the preference. What would he—*could* he say now? She tried to calm herself to meet him, but at last in desperation, she prayed:

"Oh, dear Lord, I know that all my life I've had everything, *everything,* and that I don't deserve one single thing more, and if it is Your will, I'll try to do without—him. But he loved me, I know he did, and oh, Father in Heaven, may it have been the real love so he still will love *me*. Please, dear Lord, give me just this one thing, give me David, because I love him so."

As if in answer to her prayer, she heard David's voice calling: "Cynthia, Cynthia."

"Yes, David, here I am. I—I'm fixing the rose branch, David, where it fell. I'll turn around in just a minute—as soon as I can!"

She heard his step on the path, and at last, holding tightly to the arbor gate to meet the blow when he should—see her, she turned, breathlessly. No start of surprise! His step was uncertain as he came toward her, but no change passed over his face to mar the love-light there—and suddenly Cynthia gave a half-sobbing, half-glad and half-crying start and ran into his outstretched arms. What matter if the whole world pitied her—she could meet their looks and laugh! To David Gare she would always be beautiful! *For David Gare was blind!*

THE SNOW OF
CHRISTMAS

Joseph Leininger Wheeler

*How is a story born? I don't know . . . it just comes
to you. One bitterly cold December evening in 1989,
having just turned in grades for my creative writing class,
the mood came upon me to write a Christmas story
of my own.*

Misunderstandings—every marriage is full of them. But what happens when they are permitted to grow unchecked? What then? We all know the answer: another divorce. As I looked out at the snow and ice on the river, and the cold wind shrieked as it savaged the trees, the story of a great love that was destroyed by a quarrel was born.

I sent out copies to friends. So many wrote back, thanking me and encouraging me to print it, that it proved the catalyst for putting my first story anthology together. Ten years later, the chain reaction to writing that one story resulted in my leaving the classroom and devoting the rest of my life to a ministry of Judeo-Christian stories and books. Truly there is no such thing as a small act in life.

John, Cathy, and Julie—and then there were only two.

*T*hree doors he had slammed on her: the bedroom, the front, and the car. What started it all . . . he really couldn't say; it was just one of those misunderstandings which grow up into quarrels. In a matter of minutes he had unraveled a relationship which had taken years to build. His tongue, out of control, appeared to have a life of its own— divorced as it was from his accusing mind and withdrawing heart.

"Catherine. . . . It's all been a big mistake . . . you and I. I've tried and tried—Heaven knows I've tried—but it just won't work. You're . . . you're wrong for me . . . and I'm wrong for you."

"John!"

"Don't interrupt me. I mean it. We're through. What we thought was love—wasn't. It just wasn't. . . . No sense in prolonging a dead thing. . . . Don't worry, I'll see to it that you don't suffer financially—I'll keep making the house payments. . . . And uh . . . and uh, you can keep what's in the checking and savings accounts. . . . And uh, uh, don't worry, I'll send child support for Julie!"

"John!"

Almost he came to his senses as he looked into Catherine's anguished eyes and saw the shock and the tears. But his pride was at stake, so ignoring the wounded appeal of those azure eyes, he had stormed out—his leaving punctuated with the three slammed doors.

Three weeks later, here he was, pacing a lonely motel room three thousand miles from home. Home? He had no home. He had only his job—a very good one—and his Mercedes. That's all.

Unable to face the prosecuting attorney of his mind, he turned on the TV—but that didn't help much. There were Christmas-related commercials or programming on every channel—one of these ads featured a golden-haired little girl who reminded him far too much of Julie.

He remembered Julie's wide-eyed anticipation of every Christmas. The presents under the tree, which she'd surreptitiously pick up, evaluate by weight and size and sound, and the finesse with which she unwrapped and rewrapped them . . . ; he found it hard to be stern with her for did not Catherine, too, unwrap them on the sly? Catherine had always been constitutionally unable to wait until Christmas should reveal what hid within gaily wrapped packages bearing her name—so poor Julie came about this affliction naturally.

Again, he switched channels. Wouldn't you know it: yet another Christmas special. Had to be Perry Como. . . . *still* at it. Why, the Christmas special advertised as Como's farewell performance was a number of years back—in fact, he and Catherine heard it the Christmas season of Julie's birth. . . . Como no longer had the range, but his middle range still carried him through.

Oh no! Not "I'll Be Home for Christmas". . . "You can plan on me. . . ." On the wings of Como's voice he soared backwards in time—clear back to his own childhood.

Was it his seventh Christmas . . . or his eighth? The eighth! . . . for that was the year his parents had surprised him with an adorable shaded-silver Persian kitten—which he promptly named Samantha. Samantha had lived a long time—fifteen years, in fact. And it was hard to envision life without that bundle of purring fur which cuddled up next to his feet every night—until he left for college. And even then, whenever he returned home, every night like clockwork—within sixty seconds from when he turned out the light and slipped into bed—he would sense a slight vibration resulting from the four-point landing, hear a loud purr, and feel a whiskered head searching for a head scratching.

Memories flooded in upon him in torrents now. How he had loved Christmas at home. His had always been the responsibility of decorating the Christmas tree—a tree he got to pick out himself. A REAL tree—never a fake! The fragrance of a real tree, the sticky feel of a real tree, even the shedding of a real tree . . . were all intertwined in the memories of the years.

Strange . . . passing strange . . . how he measured the passing years by specific Christmases.

The Christmas of the broken phonograph records with its now legendary "Lean-to". . . by . . . uh . . . Mari Sandoz—yeah, Sandoz wrote it. How everyone had laughed and cried over that Nebraska frontier tale. "Lean-to" had gone into the family lexicon of memories. And, as usual, all four of his grandparents had been there . . . and numerous aunts, uncles, cousins, and family friends.

Then there was the Christmas when Dad, for the first time, read *all* of Dickens's *Christmas Carol*—he had thought it would never end. But strangely, ever since that first reading, the story of Scrooge and the Cratchits seemed shorter every time it was read. And theater and movie renditions? They but reinforced the impact of the core story.

And how could he ever forget the first time he had heard Henry Van Dyke's *The Other Wise Man*? Like Dickens's tale, it normally took several evenings to read. That poignant conclusion where the dying Artaban, under the extended shadow of Golgotha, at last finds his king . . . never failed to bring tears to his eyes.

That's enough, *John! . . . . You've got to put all that behind you. Christmas? What is it but Madison Avenue's annual process of grafting sales to sentiment—that's why the first Christmas sale now takes place the day after Independence Day. . . .* But it wasn't enough: He just could not convince himself that Christmas meant no more than that. Instead, his mind flung open a door and replayed the scene in his folks' kitchen three weeks before. It had been anything but easy—rather, it had been perhaps the hardest thing he had ever done—telling them about their separation and impending divorce. And he had begged off for this Christmas, telling them that a very important business meeting on the East Coast would make his going home for Christmas impossible.

Mother had broken down when she heard about the end of his marriage, for Catherine had slipped into their hearts—becoming the daughter they had always yearned for—that first Christmas when he brought her home from college. Catherine had taken it all in: the warmth and radiance of the *real* tree; the crudely carved nativity scene (John had made it when he was twelve); the exterior Christmas lights; the Christmas decorations everywhere, the Christmas music played on the stereo and sung around the piano; the Christmas stories read during the week; the puns, jokes, kidding, and ever-present laughter; the crazy annual trading game—which was more fun than the usual exchange of presents—; the bounteous table groaning with delicious food day after day; parlor games such as Monopoly, Caroms, Dominoes, Anagrams; the crackling fire every evening; the remembering of the Christ Child; and the warmth and love that permeated every corner of the modest home.

When he had proposed—on Christmas Eve—and apologized for the plainness of the home, and compared it to the Marin County estate where she grew up . . . her eyes had blazed, and she had hushed his lips with her fingers: "Don't you *ever* apologize for your home, John! . . . There is *love* here . . . and Christ . . . and Father . . . *and* Mother—not just my lonely embittered father rattling around in all those endless rooms . . . *alone*. No, this,". . . and she paused as her gaze took it all in again, "this is the kind of home I've longed for all my life." Then her eyes, reflecting the firelight glow, softened . . . and emanated such tender, trusting love—unqualified and unreserved—that time stopped for him as he gathered into his arms what had once seemed virtually unattainable.

"This has got to stop!" he admonished himself. There can be no turning back. . . . Out of the room he strode, down the hall, down the stairs, and out into the city. It being December 23, the streets were crowded with people, all with one goal: get those last-minute gifts. He passed two Salvation Army bell ringers and left a five-dollar bill with each one.

Happiness and seasonal good humor were all around him.

Strangers wished him a very merry Christmas. Christmas carols were piped into almost every store.

His attention was caught by a crowd in front of Macy's biggest window; he pushed himself far enough in to be able to see what they were all looking at. What he saw—in a fairyland setting— was hundreds of cashmere teddy bears in varying costumes. Julie had fallen in love with them the first time she saw one (long before they had become the rage of the season). And he had planned to surprise her Christmas morning and bring it to her at the breakfast table rather than putting it under the tree. Oh, well, perhaps Catherine would remember to buy it—that is . . . which he rather doubted . . . if she was in the mood to have Christmas at all.

He moved on but seemed to feel invisible gravitational force pulling him back to Macy's. Two hours later, unable to resist any longer, he went back, bought one of the last three in stock—even the window had been cleaned out—and returned to the motel. He shook his head, not understanding in the least why he had bought it, for he was a continent away from Julie—and tomorrow was Christmas Eve.

After depositing the teddy bear in his room, he returned to the street. This time, he walked away from the downtown district. He came to a large white New England style church. The front doors were open, and floating out on the waves of night air were the celestial strains of "Ave Maria." He stopped, transfixed; then he walked up the steps and into the church. There, down candle-lit aisles to the front of the church, was a live nativity scene. And . . . off to the side . . . a lovely brunette—eyes luminous with the illusion of the moment—was singing the same song he had first heard Catherine sing, and with the same forgetfulness of self, the same intensity, and sincerity.

When she reached those last few measures and her pure voice seemed to commingle with the angels, chills went up and down his spine; and when the last note died away into infinity, there was the ultimate accolade of total silence . . . followed by a storm of applause.

John closed his eyes . . . soothed yet tormented by what he had just experienced, who the singer reminded him of, and the significance of that mother's love and sacrifice two thousand years ago.

Out of the sanctuary he strode . . . and down the street—mile after mile—until he had left even the residential district behind; on and on he walked, and did not stop until the city lights no longer kept him from seeing the stars. As he looked up into the cold December sky . . . for the first time in three traumatic weeks . . . he faced his inner self.

And he did not like what he saw.

Etched for all time in the grooves of his memory were the terrible words he had spoken to the woman he had pledged his life to. How could he have been so cruel—even if he no longer loved her? That brought him face-to-face with the rest of his life. The question, the answer, and what he would do about it, would, one way or another, dramatically affect every member of his immediate family, both now and until the day they died.

What was his answer to be?

***

It was snowing! For the first time in ten years, declared the radio announcer, there would be snow on Christmas. The windshield wipers kept time with Bing Crosby—who every December comes back to life just to sing "I'm Dreaming of a White Christmas." The lump in his throat was almost more than he could handle. Would this be a Christmas "just like the ones I used to know"? Could she—*would* she—consider taking him back?

Although bone weary from staying up all night and from the frantic search for airline reservations, he was far too tense to be sleepy. The flight had been a noisy one, and a colicky baby right behind him had ensured a wide-awake trip. He'd rented a car . . . and now . . . his heart pounded louder as each mile clicked past on the odometer.

Now that he had thrown away the most precious things in life (his wife and child), he no longer even had a home . . . and belatedly he realized that without it, life's skies for him would lose their blue. How odd that his mind meshed the graying of his personal skies with the cold-graying of Cathy's eyes: The blue of both was now as silvery as the ice- and snow-bedecked trees flashing by.

The road became icier, and he narrowly averted accidents several times. Occasionally a vehicle would spin out of control in front of him, but somehow he got around them safely.

At last! The city limits . . . he could hardly keep his runaway heart from jumping its tracks.

Had the road to his house ever seemed so long? . . . . Then . . . he turned that last corner. . . . Darkness: no lights, no car! He fought panic as he skidded into the driveway. Then he got out and fought the bitterly cold wind and snow as he stumbled to the back door. Inside, all appeared as it normally did—nothing to indicate that they had left on a long trip.

Maybe they were at his folks! He rushed back to the car, backed out onto the street, and sped out of town, hoping against hope that he was guessing right. He didn't dare to trust his fate to a telephone call.

About an hour later he saw the cheery lights of his folks' place.

Through the front window he could see the multicolored lights on the Christmas tree. And *there* . . . in the driveway, was his wife's car.

He passed the house, then circled back on an alley road, cutting his lights as he approached the house. His heart now shuddering like a jackhammer, he ever so quietly opened the back door and stepped into the gloom of the dark hall, first brushing off his clothes and shoes.

He heard a child's voice . . . singing. . . . In the darkness, he edged around the corner into the foyer. Kerosene lanterns, as always, gave to the room a dreamy serenity. His folks sat on the couch intensely watching their grandchild as she softly sang, kneeling by his nativity stable:

> *Silent night, holy night*
> *All is calm, all is bright. . . .*

A look of ethereal beauty about her, lost in her Bethlehem world.

"Oh God," he prayed, "shield her from trouble, from pain—from growing up too soon."

Then, like a sword thrust through his chest, came the realization that he—her own father—had thrust her out of that protected world children need so desperately if they are to retain their illusions, that childlike trust without which none of us will ever reach heaven's gate.

The sweet but slightly wobbly voice continued, then died away with the almost whispered:

> *Jesus, Lord at Thy birth*
> *Jesus, Lord at Thy birth.*

His heart wrenched as he drank in every inch of that frail flowering of the love he and Cathy had planted. Oh, how little it would take to blight that fragile blossom!

He wondered what his daughter had been told. . . . Would she still love him? Would she ever again trust him completely?

Upon completion of the beloved Austrian hymn, Julie sank down to the level of the nativity figures and, head propped up by elbows, gazed fixedly into another time.

John now turned to an older Julie, leaning against the window frame. She was wearing a rose-colored gown that, in the flickering light from the oak logs in the fireplace, revealed rare beauty of face and form. But her face . . . such total desolation John had never seen before. In all the long years that followed, that image of suffering was so indelibly burned into his memory . . . this heartbreak of his own making . . . that he would be unable to bury it in his subconscious.

How woebegone, how utterly weary, she appeared. A lone tear glistened as it trickled down that cheek he loved to kiss.

Oh, how he loved her!

He could hold back no longer. Silently, he approached her. Was it too late?

Suddenly, she sensed his presence and turned away from the vista of falling snow to look at him. She delayed the moment of reckoning by initially refusing to meet his eyes . . . then, very slowly, she raised her wounded eyes to his . . . and searched for an answer.

Oh, the relief which flooded over him when he saw her eyes widen as they were engulfed by the tidal wave of love that thundered across the five-foot abyss between them. In fact, it was so overwhelming that neither could ever remember how the distance was bridged—only that, through his tears, he kept saying as he crushed her to him,

"Oh, Cathy! Oh, Cathy! Forgive me, Cathy. Oh, Cathy, I love you so!"

And then there were three at the window—not counting the snow-coated teddy bear—the rest of the world forgotten in the regained heaven of their own.

And the snow of Christmas Eve continued to fall.

*If these stories of love touched your heart, you will enjoy
Joe Wheeler's other collections of timeless stories:*

HEART TO HEART STORIES OF FRIENDSHIP

A touching collection of timeless tales that will
uplift your soul. For anyone who has ever
experienced or longed for the true joy of
friendship, these engaging stories are sure to inspire
laughter, tears, and tender remembrances. Share
them with a friend or loved one.
0-8423-0586-6

HEART TO HEART STORIES FOR DADS

This collection of classic tales is sure to tug at
your heart and take up permanent residence in
your memories. These stories about fathers,
beloved teachers, mentors, pastors, and other
father figures are suitable for reading aloud to
the family or for enjoying alone for a cozy
evening's entertainment.
0-8423-3634-6

HEART TO HEART STORIES FOR MOMS

This heartwarming collection includes stories
about the selfless love of mothers, stepmothers,
surrogate mothers, and mentors. Moms in all
stages of life will cherish stories that parallel
their own, from those demonstrating the bond
between child, mother, and grandmother. A
collection to cherish for years to come.
0-8423-3603-6

CHRISTMAS IN MY HEART

Volume VIII

These stories will turn hearts to what Christmas—
and life itself—is all about. Powerful and
inspirational, each story is beautifully illustrated
with classic engravings and woodcuts, making the
collection a wonderful gift for family members
and friends. Reading these stories will quickly
become a part of any family's Christmas tradition.
0-8423-3645-1